A Racket
in the
Burbs

Ben Broeren

A Racket
in the
Burbs

Ben Broeren

Author's Note

Although *A Racket in the Burbs* is a work of fiction, the story references several actual events, including Operation Family Secrets, an FBI investigation that started in 2005 and led to the indictment of fourteen people affiliated with the Chicago mob. Any reference to the Operation is meant to give atmosphere to the fictional story and not meant to be taken as factual.

One existing mobster, Joey "the Clown" Lombardo takes a fictional role in this novel. Mr. Lombardo's dialogue herein did not take place. However, of what I did read about him thanks to research using Chicago Public Library's online databases, a cursory skimming of Jeff Coen's *Family Secrets: The Case That Crippled the Chicago Mob*, and general Google searches, I hope to represent Mr. Lombardo's character with authenticity.

The novel references several existing figures in U.S. Federal and Illinois State government. Such figures as Mike Madigan, Rod Blagojevich, Dick Cheney, and Patrick J. Fitzgerald have reputations that were well established in the national consciousness before I chose to reference them in this fictional story. My readers' opinions of how I characterize these figures will depend on which media and news sources they consume in their daily lives.

All municipal government workers, citizens, and mob figures in the fictional city of Woolrich are part of the author's informed, yet active imagination.

Salaciousness in the Suburbs

The kitsch of stained, maroon carpet and fake wood paneling coordinated rather well with the phony breasts of some of the talent onstage. Nearly two decades had passed since a Hollywood actor was U.S. President, and the decor was just as dated. Rivulets of rainbow light emanating from a silver disco ball, probably as old as some the strippers, was meant to put the clientele in fantasy mode. The lighting and butcher's block bass beats served only to accentuate the pounding in Ron McCallister's head.

This didn't help him be any more sociable than usual.

"What a complete tease...most, if not all of them are just show on the outside and hollow on the inside," he whispered sardonically to himself as he looked toward the stage of Starlet's Alley strip club. An ebony-haired, bubble gum-chewing girl was finishing her first act. "Yeah, and I'm a competent judge of character."

Ron hadn't had much luck with women in general, but seeing sultry dancers push away washed-up, bored businessmen and even sketchier characters day after day made him less compassionate toward anyone. His ambivalence, at best, and strong-arm misanthropy, at worst, started before the place he worked had last benefited from the keen eye of an interior designer.

After three decades of life, Ron still got an occasional nightmare about the origins of the one inch scar above his left eye. His father's angry glare resonated to the day. The balding, red-nosed bully had taken a cracked, black leather belt connected to a pewter buckle to make the gash on Ron's eight-year-old face. Few people could forget that.

He currently saw a man in jacket that was made with a similar quality of leather. The man had a salt and pepper goatee and the potbelly of an aging Harley Davidson enthusiast. Harley's eyes were fixed on the stage while his hands went underneath his belly to unfasten his belt. Harley wanted to do a different sort of slapping around.

Ron found an iota of release while working as a bouncer.

He tapped the wanna-be biker on the head above his shoulder and told him to get out. He was pleased when he didn't have to ask other staff to clean anything off the seat or floor after Harley zipped his fly. The public perv hurried outside to the gravel parking lot.

Ron's existence was far from glamorous to say the least, but he credited his strengths to the one person whom he loved, respected, and admired. Any physical violence from Dad stopped when she came into his life. Ron stuck to his education, which led to tours in the Army during Operation Iraqi Freedom. The realities on the other side of the world and at his one-year-old job kept him from admiring her. He had to categorize emotions to do his job well.

The next pervert Ron had to eject wasn't as clean or conscientious as Harley had been.

"Hands off the stripper," he said after noticing a customer who tried to fondle the ebony-haired stripper's ankle with a meaty paw. He grabbed the middle-aged customer. The man looked like he was trying to relive his days as an unscrupulous, frat boy at a third-rate college.

Ron almost smiled when the putz took a swing. All he needed was a reason. Customers nearby played dumb, which wasn't difficult.

"The year is 2008, well after when you would have been able to intimidate a girl to get yourself off. I'm gonna have to ask you to leave," Ron said after he intercepted the fist that had been meant for him. He proceeded to dislocate the douchebag's shoulder.

With his hand twisting the assailant's affected arm, Ron led him outside and told him to head home before the cops needed to get involved. The middle-aged frat boy winced as he made his way to a waiting taxicab.

Despite the crackling of adrenaline, Ron's fuse fizzled as he went back in to the club. The confusion was made more opaque when he saw Carey Sullivan take the stage. Somehow, the lack of clarity didn't aggravate him as much as strike him with awe.

Ron's mind drifted when Carey took off her sequined bra to show the awestruck audience the healthy natural breasts swaying above her curvy hips and slender waist. The catchy bass line from Justin Timberlake's "Rock Your Body" ricocheted in his head like fire from a semiautomatic assault rifle. His eyes took in the smooth skin on her petite frame. He didn't have a problem with her. She was friendly, always saying "hello" to him every day they worked together.

The thing that did worry him was when thoughts of Carey interrupted time outside of work when he was trying to be numb. When Ron saw her dance five or six days out of the week, he became less hostile than usual. He became more like a scared child than an angry hoodlum, not that the two personality types were mutually exclusive.

Carey made Ron feel vulnerable, which could make him either sweet or tough. His job required that he be more of the latter. He wasn't as comfortable with being sweet. At least that's what he rationalized to himself while he tried to keep his eyes off of the button nose between Carey's hazel eyes.

Walls are a good thing in this business...keep looking for johns and losers, Ron thought. His boss not-so-gently interrupted with what was supposed be a cordial clip on his right shoulder.

"That's a nice piece of ass, ain't she?" asked Sal Paretti, the owner of Starlet's Alley. "I first thought you was a fag until I noticed you taking in her curvy bits. That Sullivan chick's got the sincere vibe of innocence. It makes men want to either drop their drawers or empty their wallets. Since she doesn't meet them to drop their drawers, it's even better for business. The idiots always think they got a chance..."

Asshole, Ron thought before denying his interest in her.

"I just like to be a professional," he said. "I'm also not a fan of venereal disease. I learned enough about the clap when I was slaving away for Uncle Sam in the second Bush's Gulf War. I was told the innocent-looking ones are the most dangerous."

"Say, did you kill any of those Arabs?" Paretti asked after trying to stick his chest past his belly. "I'm a hot-blooded American and appreciate your service if you did."

Ron had to take a minute to let the stupid

comment slide.

I'd gladly snap your neck if you want me to, he thought. *But then I'd have to hide the body, find a new job...*

Ron hoped for an opportunity to divert his attention from the imbecile who paid him. He hated his boss, but he was somewhat amused by the pride the grease ball took in running such a joint in Chicago's western suburb of Woolrich. Paretti enjoyed his coveted status as a local business owner.

Ron found it easier to distract himself with anger than dissect other more unguarded emotions. He focused on the local dregs of society, some of whom only differed by dressing better.

Starlet's Alley was supposedly the only locally owned money-making establishment in their suburb. There was St. Francis Catholic Church and St. Paul Presbyterian, which Ron also considered money-making establishments, albeit not locally owned. Woolrich also had a Burger King, a Hooters, and a newish Walmart among chains that their mayor said would bring "hundreds of new jobs to our beloved city."

Ron figured most of his neighbors knew that city government wasn't really run by locals either, what with its allegiance to whatever the state legislature wanted. State government officials were frequent clients of Starlet's Alley. He knew which politician preferred which special stripper.

Woolrich's mayor, George De Silva, gave his boss at Starlet's Alley a tax break to keep the fine, local small business in their armpit of a town. For such benevolence from local political patronage, Ron was paid three times what those poor bastards at Walmart where making.

Well-dressed assholes are still repulsive, Ron thought.

He smiled when he thought he saw Carey's eyes glance at his own before she left the stage. As his smile faded, he took stock of the time and realized that it would be five more hours before he could get a bit drunk before hitting his bed.

I've got to shut down my mind and get to my job, Ron thought as a busty blonde with the nickname "Gonzagas" came out to a Britney Spears song. He reverted to a robotic efficiency of ass-kicking when he realized what he had to do to a customer who was threatening one of the bartenders.

Two weeks into spring and the frisky shit bags are gonna make it a busy night.

- - - - -

Carey Sullivan didn't really enjoy how everyone liked to watch her flaunt her breasts and her hips. Still, she didn't raise a fuss as long as she got enough green to take care of her three-year-old son, John. She did almost whatever it took to keep him out of trouble or debt, even if she had to make lonely businessmen and perverts play lecherous hands. As long as she could collect the green and not offer any bedroom antics, she wouldn't call their bluffs. She would never let them win the jackpot of a night with her.

John's biological sperm donor skipped town after Carey told him she was pregnant. The miscreant even took $200 she kept hidden in a fake wall in a closet of her one-bedroom apartment. This proved her uncanny ability to find and keep untrustworthy men. She didn't have much time to find a good companion while showing her goods to happy hour hangers-on with stained t-shirts and leisure suits.

Well, at least these douchebags give me money instead of stealing it, she thought. *If I have to flash my assets to make a profit, so be it.*

The one guy who she found interesting was the only guy who seemed to have little interest in her except when she was on stage. She couldn't really understand why he was so quiet and moody. She wasn't spring chicken material at thirty-one years of age, but her friends outside the Alley still said she could pull off the studious, yet flirtatious, grad student look.

Carey appreciated that friends who didn't work at the club complimented her on her looks and helped with John. The interesting bouncer, Ron McCallister, only gave her a curt nod when she said "hello" to him every day. She supposed that he could be gay, but their boss, Sal Paretti wouldn't hire a twink, even if it would be a good business decision.

Officially Paretti was a devout Catholic who admired Pope Benedict and regularly gave a tithing to the local parish.

Anyway, if McCallister isn't gay, maybe he just doesn't like redheads, she thought. *At least he makes sure wanna-be Casanovas keep their hands to themselves.*

She reminded herself that she didn't have time to worry about the unfriendly bouncer tonight or most other nights. She had enough on her plate to keep her busy with her son. She still couldn't deny that she found Ron kind of cute in the same way teenage girls fawned over a brooding Morrisey in the late 1980s.

Jesus, more complexity is all I damned well

need, Carey thought as she gyrated her naked hips on a pole to applauding men desperate for her attention. *These jokers tossing dollar bills my way won't be able to screw me in any other way*.

Carey grew cynical when she thought about life in Woolrich. She could choose to focus on that, her son, or the good-looking, albeit moody bouncer. One topic depressed her, the other topic was unfit for a strip club, and she tried to shut her mind off from Ron as she pressed her cleavage to the pole. She squatted at the end of her second song, Prince's "Purple Rain," and tried to remain numb. As her moves got more fluid, the depressing crowd likely found it sensuous.

"I loathe you," she mouthed at a businessman, changing her lips to reflect love instead of hate. She was glad no one was perceptive enough to know the difference and give less of a tip. She still had to make a living.

Carey glanced at her co-worker, Ron. She was surprised and pleased by his slight smile, but she had to keep up her act. Her swaying hips teased everyone who was watching her leave the stage. She had no intention of indulging the fantasies of depressing men when she wasn't on stage..

- - - - -

Mayor George De Silva snorted a smudge of cocaine from between Skyla's breasts before he downed a shot of Grey Goose Vodka. He took pride in his feeling of control over his wife, Anne, their three kids, and the city of Woolrich. But enjoying party tricks courtesy of his friend, Sal Paretti, was what really made him tick. Cocaine and the sex-for-hire only pumped up his blimp-sized ego to the point of popping.

As the powder from Skyla's breasts burned

his sinuses, he tried to reassure himself that he had it all. He wasn't even focused on the buoyantly busty blonde in front of him. A sudden paranoia fueled his compulsion for self-pity. This, in turn, kept him from completely enjoying his chemical euphoria and the big globes of silicone before him. De Silva became the opposite of what what he wanted to portray politically. He decided to be petty and boring.

He was pissed that some of the reporters at the *Chicago Sun-Times* didn't cut him any slack. He wanted control over public opinion, as well. His problem was that the public couldn't be entirely bought. Voters still read newspapers, even one that was losing money and subscribers every year.

If a newspaper is constantly battling bankruptcy, then how can they be trusted? Mayor De Silva thought. *I'm all about the truth, as long as it reflects the market. The business markets reflect the greatest truth after all. At least TV news is more likely to do what they're damned well told.*

Mayor De Silva began sneezing almost uncontrollably after his last snort of coke. Despite his attempts to get high and make a bimbo service him, he was preoccupied with politics and press reports. He was angry that the public continually failed to notice his attempts to reach out to the community.

He pushed Skyla onto the ground as he ran his hands through his increasingly thinning hair. He took another shot of vodka in a weak attempt to calm down his focus on frustrations. Skyla just lit a Newport Menthol Light cigarette, limped over to the bed and started pleasing herself to pass the time. Her john had to take some time to recoup his stamina.

And so De Silva continued to pout.

Sal Paretti was the biggest local supporter and recipient of De Silva's political-economic orchestrations. Not only did he lavish the mayor with illicitly contracted working girls and blow, but the owner of Starlet's Alley was his strongest advocate for moral character when election season came around. Favors went both ways as the mayor turned a blind eye toward the strip club's after hours cocaine sales.

Political ties put an end to Planned Parenthood when it tried to establish itself in Woolrich. Paretti and De Silva made sure it was dead on arrival with a combination of "public indignation" and "incorrect application procedure with respect to municipal zoning laws."

"This city will not and can not turn its back on traditional values," the mayor had said. To his credit, over half the city's voters believed he wasn't being fake.

God bless democracy, Mayor De Silva thought as he caught his breath and shook his head. He smiled as he noticed what Skyla was doing. *It can be bought for less than a dictatorship. Ignorance and apathy are more valuable currencies than guns.*

The mayor's thoughts were far from the rest of his family. He didn't let anything bother him when he joined his paid company in the bed he was supposed to be sharing with with wife. Skyla put out her cigarette on the hickory headboard and got back to her professional duties with the quickness of a coked-up turtle.

Mayor De Silva's two sons were on the other side of their mansion. Fraternal twins, Tom and Bryan, were arguing over whether to get the newest iPhone or Android for their upcoming thirteenth birthday. His daughter, Kendra, was supposedly out studying. Her mother, Anne, suspected she was doing drugs much more unpredictable than weed with her other seventeen-year old classmates from Poynter Prep. But Mayor De Silva really didn't care about any concerns his wife had. He was almost a worse father than he was a husband.

- - - - -

In the adjacent room, Anne naively thought she was the only one aware of her husband's recreational activities as she tried to read the latest Nora Roberts novel to distract herself. She gave up when she heard the creaks from the king-sized bed and the porn-inspired fake moans coming out of Skyla's mouth. She had had enough.

Three bangs from a Ruger .44 semiautomatic handgun abruptly put their mansion in an eerie silence until police arrived just after two that morning.

After the gunshots, Anne left with the twins in a well-tracked Jeep Cherokee. It wasn't long before police would find her and separate her from her kids.

She was more shocked than anyone to be arrested on suspicion of her husband's death.

2

Day In, Day Out

Ron McCallister woke up with the same pounding headache that he had the night before. Then again, he usually woke up with a jackhammer to his head due to his habit of drinking several shots of Evan Williams after work. As he got up from his mattress an hour before noon, he hoped that the construction crew in his cerebellum would soon take a smoke break. This would at least make the start of his daily workout more pleasant. Before he began, he took three ibuprofen with tap water, filled his electric kettle, and turned it on.

He did fifty sit-ups in two minutes and followed with just as many push-ups before putting three tablespoons of Great Value Classic Roast and scalding hot water in his French press coffee maker. A pleasant leather and berry aroma permeated the six hundred square feet of his studio apartment. As endorphins, the anti-inflammatory meds, and caffeine quickly took over, he began to feel much better.

The simple, tan brick building in which he lived housed one-bedroom and two-bedroom apartments as well, but Ron didn't need that much space. He had a futon, a fridge, and a General Electric stove to make mac and cheese, frozen veggies, frozen fish, and the occasional pot roast on which he could live for a week. From his one window he could see the Walmart, which made him feel peaceful for some reason.

My asshole boss, Paretti, at least pays me more than those poor jokers, he thought. *I can afford to be a good customer.*

After a quick breakfast of generic Cheerios, a banana, two hard boiled eggs and whole milk to go along with his coffee, he did ten pull-ups before washing his six-foot frame in his three-foot by three-foot shower. He donned a black t-shirt and bluejeans before sitting down to read the *Sun-Times*. Apparently, the early morning hours had been rough for their mayor, and the newspaper probably didn't have much more depth than the police report, save for humanizing touches from neighbors and "friends."

Woolrich's finest rent-a-cops found a bloody hooker along with the slain mayor, and Anne De Silva was arrested on suspicion of the double homicide. She claimed total innocence, of course. The mayor's twin boys, Tom and Bryan, were at an aunt's house in Cicero. His daughter, Kendra, hadn't been located as of press time.

It was not that Ron really gave a damn what happened to the mayor, but he was sure to get an earful of conspiracy theories from his well-connected boss when he got to work. At least he'd have some hours of peace and quiet before starting his shift at four thirty.

After Ron was done with the local news, gave a casual glance at the sports page, and cleaned his kitchenette, he opened a Dashiell Hammett novel, Red Harvest. He had the hard-boiled classic on loan from the closest public library in Naperville. He enjoyed its story of a private dick taking on municipal corruption and the mob.

Woolrich might be dirty, but not like this, he thought as he read. *I doubt any of the local schmucks would be so well-organized.*

At quarter to four, he finished another cup of coffee and put down the book. He decided to take a leisurely walk to Starlet's Alley. He figured that once at work, he would have to get back to dispensing with any riffraff that got in the way of business.

- - - - -

Backstage at Starlet's Alley, Carey Sullivan put on her Velcro-fastened, thigh-slit, black pencil skirt and tied a skimpy white blouse to teasingly conceal her breasts. She knew that it was one of Sal Paretti's favorites and she was looking for a slight raise to make things easier for John and herself. She figured the nearly translucent top and hardened bits underneath would help with negotiations.

She took solace in the fact that she didn't have worry about her sons immediate needs at work. Her most trustworthy friend outside the strip club, Lizzy Simmons, tended to her son during shifts as a stripper. Lizzy was a stay-at-home mother and wife of a man with a good City Hall job in communications. Their son, Brian, was slightly older than John.

Any sense of zen about her day was shattered when Carey overheard Paretti talking to Ron while walking by his office.

"I don't wanna see anyone," he said as she straightened her blouse "My boy got a bullet to the head and the deputy mayor, Rob Peck, presents himself as some kind of reformer. I've gotta help him get realistic, and that's gonna make a lot of extra work when I should be mourning a friend."

So today might not be the day to ask for a raise, Carey thought. She had heard about the deaths in the mayor's mansion on WGN news, but she hadn't made the connection with how that might affect Paretti's mood. Her mind had been focused on her kid.

All she could do for the night was strut out in a seductive but not-so-pretend irritated way and hope the customers were in a better mood. If not, she'd be flaunting her curves and gyrating her hips for a little less bread until she got everyone warmed up. She figured that she'd need at least another year of tempting customers but didn't have much time to plan a future outside of Woolrich.

Might as well get this shit show on the road and make some money, Carey thought as she psyched herself up.

The larger than average crowd exploded as she swayed her hips and cut one foot in front of the other on stage. After the house deejay filled the room with the bass drum-laden, finger-tapping guitar intro to Van Halen's "Hot for Teacher," Carey focused on the strength in her legs as she squatted and ripped off her skirt before standing.

She focused on the job while raising herself with her chiseled arms to a pole connected from stage to ceiling. She drew into herself when she clenched the pole between her hamstring and calf muscles before swinging round. David Lee Roth's vocals echoed the lasciviousness of the dozens gathered beneath her.

- - - - -

The Sicilian ordinarily considered himself a friend of people like the late mayor. The Armani-clad thug shared De Silva's interest in strip clubs, cocaine, and getting serviced by someone who was not a wife or girlfriend. But business was business, especially when expansion got threatened by sloppiness and increasingly tenuous political clout. Chicago mob insiders sent him to clean things up and get more control of the burbs.

It's good to have influence over Woolrich police and give them perks, he thought. *It's even better that the Chicago* famiglia *has paid help in the Feds, the Illinois legislature, and beyond. We'll get along better with our current mayor.*

He almost laughed about the fact that Anne De Silva was getting screwed by the legal system in the same way her late husband had been screwing her: not pleasantly.

He could have taken out her and the kids too, but then the setup wouldn't be as believable. Anne wouldn't earn a mother-of-the-year award, but she wouldn't kill her kids. He preferred not to kill anyone under eighteen.

The Sicilian had also been a father at one point. He didn't like to think about his daughter because it brought up the painful memory of her getting shot dead by an overzealous cop. His only solace was the slow and painful death that the cop was given courtesy of salt and dull knives.

At 5-foot-10, the Sicilian wasn't exactly a physically intimidating specimen. But what he lacked in size, he made up for in malevolence and accuracy with high powered handguns. He cleaned his Ruger .44 semiautomatic and sipped a Pinot Grigio while he dialed for a high-priced Chicago call girl. He'd gladly pay an extra fee for transporting her to the burbs.

Exercise and moderate drinking are good for the heart, after all, he thought. *Can't worry about expenses when it comes to my health.*

3

Grimy Hands, Good Hearts

Ron woke up earlier than usual because he had a day off from work. After his late morning of exercise, French press coffee, a Don Miguel breakfast burrito, and three ibuprofen, he popped over to Walmart to do some shopping.

Due to the warming weather of early spring, he wore only a light rain coat over his usual black T-shirt and jeans. He picked up a dogwood silk flower arrangement and a deck of cards before heading to Woolrich Metra Station. At a liquor store along the way, he bought a pint of Jameson to bring to his last tie to humanity. He was in a better mood than usual because he could visit the lady he had to mentally separate from the profanity of daily life.

He boarded the 1:11 p.m. Burlington Northern Santa Fe Metra line toward Naperville. The uncomfortable train afforded him the polite grins of older ladies and the ambivalence of the well-tailored yuppie set. The thing he found most annoying were the deafening cries of over-sugared, five and six-year-old kids who should have been in school. He put in earplugs and braced himself for the 17 minute, 43 second ride westward to Naperville. He walked the one and a half miles to Lavender Springs Hospice rather than brave any screaming kids on Pace buses.

A strange combination of moldy and antiseptic smells pervaded Ron's nostrils as he entered the hospice. He dutifully signed in and showed his identification to the bored-looking, gray-haired front desk lady before moseying cautiously down a narrow, jaundice-colored tile hallway to room 15b. At the entrance, his usually stoic face brightened into a natural grin as he met his maternal aunt.

"Aunt Peggy, I would have brought real dogwoods, but these pot-lickers can't be trusted to take care of flowers if they can barely give my aunt what she needs," he said. "How are you feeling? I brought you other gifts that may make you smile."

"Well, kiddo, the lung cancer hasn't killed me yet, so I doubt these jokers could hurt me," she said. "A decade ago, I could've kicked all their duffs. I'm glad you came before Jeopardy or Wheel of Fortune. You don't need to bring anything else grand except yourself."

The two hundred square foot space that surrounded his shrinking Aunt Peggy desperately needed the flowers, even though they were fake. The off-white walls, 18.5-inch TV, tray table, and bulky, wooden guest chair reminded Ron more of a sanitarium than a place of rest. Aunt Peggy lifted her pale, veined arms slightly before Ron took the hint and gave her a soft embrace and a peck on the forehead.

"I brought cards, if you got your cribbage board," he said.

"Thank God you finally learned how to play," she replied. "I'm getting rather sick of watching the idiot box. I otherwise have to wait 'til my old pal, Ervin, comes from down the hall to get any games in. I can't reach my board on account of keeping it hidden from some of the thieving nurses."

"How's Ervin doing? I thought the docs only gave him only two weeks?" Ron said as he reached under the bed's mattress to retrieve the board and set up a game. He dealt and kept

score for both of them. He always let her lead
with crib.

"Well, he's getting a little bit slower in the
head on account of his brain tumor and that
damn China-man doctor not upping his
morphine. They always underestimate him
because he's a Negro, but he's a tough old
bugger and a good cribbage buddy. If we weren't
on death's door, I might give the cocoa a try...By
the way, you better give me the whole sixteen
points for this double double run of three. Hurry
up and count your hand first, dear."

Aunt Peggy was one of the only people who
could get Ron to blush. After he groaned in mock
embarrassment and counted his hand, he
dutifully moved her peg the sixteen paces. He
brought out the pint of Jameson and poured
them each a few fingers in Styrofoam coffee
cups as she counted her crib. He positioned a
straw for her before adding more points.

"Don't get all touchy with me 'cause I talk to
you like a grown-up," she said before sipping the
whiskey and flashing what remained of her teeth
in a smile. "You ought to find somebody while
you're young. A handsome man like you oughta
find yourself a nice, fit gal."

Ron nodded respectfully as he felt another
blush. His mild embarrassment was infinitely
more bearable than a soon-to-be future without
her.

"Unless you're one of those funny fellas who's
into the other fellas. But who'm I to judge? I
don't get how it works for the gays though. How
do those fellas have kids? How do those gals who
like other gals make whoopee?"

Ron smiled at the ability of his aunt to mix
the serious with the silly. He reminded her that

he already told her how gays and lesbians do it.

She shrugged and gave a wry grin.

"I've witnessed enough from my own father and mother to not want to get involved with any steady gal," Ron said. "And no, I'm not into the fellas."

"Bah, not that hooey again. Your pa wasn't half the man you grew up to be. After your ma passed, I told him that I'd shoot him if he hit you again. And there you go, did he ever try to hit you again?"

Aunt Peggy's got a point, he thought.

"And you can do a lot better. The key is to find someone who'll be kind without me threatening to shoot 'em," she said. She winked when Ron grinned.

Ron and Aunt Peggy chuckled and carried on with their games and prattle about family, the past, and subjects they didn't talk about with anyone else. After a few refills of Jameson, Aunt Peggy had skunked him twice. He thought she let him win the last time before he stashed the cribbage board for future enjoyment.

"You work at one of those places where the girls take their clothes off, don't you?" she asked rhetorically. "Don't be too surprised if one of those gals is smarter and kinder than she lets on. Some people just got troubles. If not the strip joint, there's always cute gals at churches. I won't get into trying to get you to be Catholic again, but they also do fun stuff outside of church. The first time I got pissed up was at a church picnic. The beer was free, so there is that."

Ron gave a wink and a smile before responding.

"I know you want me to get out and have

more fun," he said. "Frivolity is a hard thing for me to grasp. I need to find my own direction."

Aunt Peggy nodded knowingly before pointing toward her cup. Her nephew dutifully got out the Jameson and poured her another dram. He cut himself off before they turned on the TV.

He watched her beat the defending Jeopardy champion and guide a Wheel of Fortune contestant to victory. He then gave her a forehead massage before pecking her on the cheek and promising to return in a week.

"Next time, you ought to bring a girlfriend around," she said. "If you need an excuse to figure out any of your hangups, do it for your Aunt Peggy. I ain't got all the time in the world, you know."

Ron blew a kiss goodbye, knowing that she could be gone in a matter of weeks. He tried to keep the thought of losing her from his mind.

"I love ya, Aunt Peggy," he said.

"Always," she replied. "Always."

Goddamn it, it's not always about me, he thought while walking slowly back to the Metra. He'd have to put on his polite face for the ride home.

After a few miles to his apartment, it was time for Dashiell Hammett and a dram or three of Evan Williams. Sleep didn't come easily, but his mind and body eventually lost consciousness.

- - - - -

Carey Sullivan turned the corner with John after she picked him up at Lizzy's, house. It was half past eleven in the evening, which was early for her. Business was slower with the latest scandal involving the late the Mayor De Silva and his family.

As she walked toward her very used Toyota

Corolla, she noticed a disheveled, teenage girl wandering north of a small park. The girl was dressed in a torn, pink tube top and a short jean skirt. Her unsteady gait hinted that the teenager was either stoned, lost, or hurt.

Carey knew that she should just shrug off the stranger and continue about her business, but many things about the girl reminded her of herself at that age, defiant despite fleeing from disappointment to disappointment. She stopped when her motherly instincts got the upper hand.

"You seem a ways from home, hon. Do you need any help?" she asked.

"Go away," the teenager said. "I don't rely on asshole adults."

"Well that's fine, if you want. I'll just take my son home and heat up some food before turning in. But if you don't need anything, I'll just report your description to the police and sleep in my clean, full-sized bed."

Carey was almost to her car before the scantily-clad teenager stopped her with a pleading look on her gaunt face.

"Sorry, I'd like a place to stay if possible," the teenager said. "I ran out of luck and would really appreciate any help."

"You should ditch the street-rat vibe more often," Carey said. "You'll get farther that way. I'll give you a place to stay tonight because I've been in rough spots myself. After that, you gotta figure something out for the long term."

"Thank you."

"By the way, what should I call you? After all, you will be staying at my apartment for a night and eating the little food that I have for me and my son."

"Kendra, ma'am."

"Get in. I'm Carey and my little man's name is
John," she said before strapping John in the back
seat. They drove in silence the two miles home.

At Carey's one-bedroom apartment, Kendra
was lent a spare Chicago Fire t-shirt, clean
sheets, and a couch in the living room. After
Carey tucked John in her bedroom, the two
women dined on some reheated KFC in relative
silence within the sparsely-lit walls of the living
space.

After eating, Carey bade her guest goodnight
and went to her room to join her son to get a
fitful sleep. After stripping into her underwear
and a t-shirt, she left her purse, containing
anything valuable, attached to a bell on the
dresser to the left of her bed.

Carey was generous from time to time, but
not stupid.

4

Gunshots, Mobsters and Kung Fu at the Strip Club

The small jingle of the bell attached to her purse was imperceptible to most people in the peacefulness of sleep, but it rattled Carey Sullivan. In one smooth, three-second motion, she retrieved the Beretta. 22 compact handgun from underneath her pillow, released the safety, cocked the gun, and pointed it at Kendra.

Kendra didn't see the gun pointed at her in the dim, early morning light just barely filtering through the blinds, but the unmistakable click made her freeze in place. The blush and tense features on her face showed fear that she had made a dumb mistake.

"Talk about a shitty way to pay someone back," Carey confidently said. "I recognize you from the news after I slept on the idea a bit. You're the dead mayor's daughter. Police couldn't find you after your pop was killed. I just demand that you put that money back in my purse and quietly get the hell out of my apartment."

Carey noticed her unwelcome guest's brief look of shock before the teenage delinquent dropped the cash and mustered a direct, defiant glare that was probably meant to be threatening.

"You're not really going to shoot the mayor's daughter are you, gutter trash?" Kendra hissed with all the snottiness she could summon. "I didn't hear that my dear old dad was dead. I ain't devastated at that discovery. I've probably got quite a bit of money coming to me."

"Jeez, you really are a cold-hearted bitch, aren't you? You ought to be taught a lesson, but I don't want to further mess up my son's sleep."

Carey pulled on a robe as she leveled the gun at Kendra's abdomen. She started to dial 911 as the teenage wanna-be thief pulled out her iPhone.

Although Kendra had a gun pointed at her and the cops on the other end of Carey's telephone line, she didn't appear too concerned. With a stern, commanding voice, Kendra phoned someone who could ostensibly help her, giving Carey's address. She ended the call with a few salutations in Italian.

Carey decided against getting the police involved and hung up just as her call was answered. She didn't want to report any guns, theft, or other affairs. In the courts, it would be her word against a dead mayor's daughter. The man was reputed through gossip and press allegations to have cops in his pocket.

"I don't care who you called," Carey said. "Take my t-shirt off, put your skank top back on, and get out of my house. Now!"

"You really don't have many bargaining chips except for that gun. And that isn't much of one unless you want harassment by police and professional hit men. But this is getting boring, and I've no interest in dealing with child protective services, either. So I think I'll just take your shirt, your bottle of Jack, and hit the road. By the way, the generic corn flakes you have suck."

Kendra hurried to get out of the bedroom, grabbing the fifth of Jack she'd found in an upper cupboard before going out the front door. She dropped the bottle after Carey fired a round from her Beretta into the ground spread between them. Gunshots in the early morning were not a noticeable rarity on this side of town.

Carey was almost laughing when she locked the screaming, red-faced debutante out of the apartment. She was more intrigued when two stocky, olive-skinned men got out of a Ford Mustang and escorted the tantrum-throwing tramp to the back seat. The peculiar thing was that they weren't threatening. They seemed to be rather deferential.

"There's a kid who needs to get a damn job," she said. She headed back to her bedroom to comfort John and try to get a few more hours of shuteye before work.

A sense of peace didn't come easily.

- - - - -

Ron McCallister yawned five hours into his shift at Starlet's Alley. The lights, spinning disco ball and crappy techno between strippers usually annoyed him. Now they just faded into walls that had been stained with cigarette smoke before the state-wide ban took effect the previous January. He grabbed a Red Bull at the bar and willed himself to be vigilant. It was easier when he heard Axl Rose shrieking over the old-school speaker system with "Welcome to the Jungle." The show was about to start.

Those two customers are flashers, gunmen, perverts or all of the above, Ron thought as he watched the two olive-skinned, musclebound goombahs enter with bulges in their black trench coats. *They aren't subtle at any rate.*

Starlet's Alley, as a policy, didn't check potential customers for concealed weapons. The rationale was that customers wouldn't be persuaded to keep things peaceful and legal by tough-looking but unarmed bouncers. Frisking someone would only be a provocation. Ron still decided to pay the trench coats a lot of attention. He was thinking of innocent-looking ways to provoke a reaction.

"Look at those greasy queers," Sal Paretti said to him as the trench coats sat down in front of the stage. "They may look Italian, but those twinks are more accustomed to the Greek than the Roman lifestyle. If they make any rash moves, don't hesitate to ask them to leave. Politely, if you can."

"No problem, boss," Ron said with a grin. "I'm always polite and I'm sure these two will appreciate that."

The sarcasm was lost on Paretti. Ron tapped his toe to Axl Rose's vocals and Slash's riffs as he waited for the one gal in the joint who piqued his interest. The intro to "Hot for Teacher" was the cue.

Carey Sullivan came out on the stage dressed in a familiar pencil skirt and white button-down. She wore conservative black pumps at the end of her muscular, nylon-clad legs. Ron enjoyed the slit in her skirt before quickly moving his eyes to more polite areas. The dark red locks framing her face were held in a bun by number-two pencils. There was a slight blush on her otherwise alabaster cheeks.

Ron had to work hard not focus on Carey's delicious curves. He noticed his overly-dressed targets were staring at her as well, despite Paretti's usually stupid assumptions. One ran a hand over a hairless head as the other creep with curly black hair eyed her toned thigh.

Ron decided to pay them a non-threatening visit and ask them if wait staff could get them some drinks. He was met by fast-paced Italian, but he did make out orders for a dirty Sapphire

Martini and a Maker's Mark Manhattan. When he returned with their drinks, straight-up, he wasn't expecting a thank you, but they didn't offer any payment, let alone gratuity.

"*Prego*," Ron replied as he handed them a bill.

They only returned angry glares, so he decided to give them a little test as Carey shrugged her unfastened blouse off her creamy shoulders. Testosterone raged through his system as the vision of Carey made him more cocky. She looked vulnerable, which made her seem more sensuous.

Dammit, she's looking me in the eyes and looks sexy as hell, Ron thought. *Think I'll get a reaction from some crude customers.*

Ron got an ice water from the bar and fake stumbled while going past the trench coat-clad tough guys. He didn't spill on them but soaked the table. As he feigned hurry to get a mop and clean up, the stocky bastards had the gall to go after him. All he needed was a reason to get rough. He deftly dodged a right jab from the hairless hooligan.

The thug lacking hair yelped after Ron grabbed his left arm and bent it behind his back, nearly pulling it out of its socket. The curly-haired creep grabbed a wooden chair and started swinging it. Ron gave the chair a roundhouse kick, busting it into a few pieces. The crowd seemed to enjoy the violence that went along with their booze and the gorgeous, topless redhead on stage.

Christ, the crowd's really eating up this show, Ron thought before the hairless hooligan whipped out a stiletto switchblade and started swinging toward him. Ron quickly grabbed part of the broken chair and knocked both the switchblade and the bald goon to the ground.

The fun ended when the thug with curly hair pulled out a Beretta .45 semiautomatic handgun from his shoulder holster. He aimed it at Ron's chest.

The few customers that were there on a weekday rushed toward the exit as Ron and the curly-haired creep squared off. Paretti was shouting for Ron to back off when a vision in their periphery changed the equation.

Carey jumped off the stage and cold-cocked the curly-haired thug in the skull with one of the pumps that had been on her feet. Unfortunately for Ron, the shooter squeezed off a round that nicked his left shoulder. Still, it was better than a shot to the heart.

Paretti sneaked away as chaos filled Starlet's Alley. One of Ron's fellow bouncers dialed for the ambulance as Carey put pressure on his wound. The hairless hooligan, meanwhile, slowly got up and took his partner's Beretta. He then put an explosive round into his curly-haired co-worker's head and was stopped before putting a round into Ron or Carey.

The other bouncer pointed a Glock semiautomatic at the Beretta-toting assailant while on the phone. The Glock was taken from behind the bar.

The hairless hooligan left to avoid tangling with the bouncer and before the requisite police presence arrived. He quickly drove his Ford Mustang away from the club as sirens could be heard in the distance.

- - - - -

The hairless hooligan didn't have long to live after he returned to his boss' three-story greystone house in Naperville. The Sicilian saw to it that his underling reported exactly what went on at the strip joint. The boss let his Associate, a very recent hire, slowly carve out a confession with a dull, three inch steak knife. The mask on the face of his recent-hire scared the bald baddie and kept the identity of his torturer a secret.

One has to dole out such brutalities to maintain order, the Sicilian thought. *Any of those under me should prefer to die rather than to leave a job unfinished. Now I gotta clean things up and be the boss.*

The hairless hooligan screamed for more than four minutes as he spewed out all the information in his head. The Associate finally put the bald thug out of his misery with a slash to his windpipe. The sudden silence was far from serene.

The Sicilian then ordered that a so-called accident happen at Carey Sullivan's rental. It was to burn to the ground, hopefully with her inside it. He didn't really want her son to be burned in it. There were some lines he felt, in his gut, uncomfortable crossing.

Sometimes you gotta cross that line to make sure a spunky bitch doesn't get out of line, he thought. *As long as the head doesn't keep track of what the right hand needs to do...*

Fortunately for his small scrap of scruples, an available gap-toothed goon was able to be his arsonist and blissfully ignorant right hand. The Associate's cruelty was better harnessed as a tool to induce fear that would get less notice from the media.

The Sicilian would have tried to send an assassin to Woolrich Memorial Hospital to take out Ron McCallister, but he figured that there was too much excitement for that. If the fire didn't kill Carey, he'd have to put her and Ron six feet under soon enough in a way that wouldn't draw unwanted attention.

The mob's plans need finesse, he thought. *That's something that those two goons I sent to the strip joint didn't practice. I will have to buy off a good number of higher-ups to muddy the waters. More disappearances are bound to happen.*

5

Hangover

Ron woke up with a worse headache than he had on most mornings after a post-work whiskey snack. Instead of a jackhammer to his head, he felt like squirrels were using tiny cleavers on his skull as if searching for goodies in an oversize walnut. This, despite the cooling sensation of a morphine drip that made him more slap-happy than numb.

The next thing he noticed was that he been out for at more than a day since his most recent shift at Starlet's Alley. He figured this out from the marked-up generic calendar on the beige wall. He said a four-letter word to himself when he couldn't wipe the drool that he knew was on his chin. His arms were restrained to the bed.

How in the hell did that happen? All I did to get in here was do my job, he thought with a throbbing head.

He remembered two olive-skinned tough guys getting violent after he had splashed some water near them. He had to rough them up a bit when they started throwing up punches. The hairless hooligan pulled out a knife. The curly-haired creep pulled out a hand cannon and squeezed a round off to nick his left shoulder, which didn't hurt as much as his head.

Ron also remembered that the redhead stripper with the curves, Carey, had stunned the guy with the gun, which was really why he was still having these thoughts. He recalled that a quick-thinking bouncer had staved off any future shots and called for help. He didn't know where any of these characters were at the moment, but he knew he had to get the hell out of dodge before anyone who had ordered the restraints returned. Fortunately enough for him, the staff had used leather restraints rather than handcuffs.

There wasn't really a place for him to go, as whoever armed the two tough guys was likely casing his studio apartment. The police were probably keeping an eye out too, for that matter.

One damned thing at a time, eh, McCallister? he thought. *Ignore the sadistic squirrels in your cerebellum, get out of bed, find some clothes, and figure out the rest.*

Ron strained his right wrist against the restraints, moving lower on the guard rail of the bed to see if he could locate where the restraint was fastened. He considered himself fortunate that he had heard about a similar escape by one of the patients at Lavender Springs Hospice. The guy had been supposedly diagnosed a delusional schizophrenic, but he still got out of his restraints before staff tased him in the parking lot. Aunt Peggy befriended him after the episode and introduced him to her nephew.

It's lovely how we treat our seniors, he thought as he calmly unsnapped his right arm. *Now with the left.*

After Ron swung his legs to the ground, he took some time to let the squirrels in his head stop humping. He was careful not to disturb the monitors of his oxygen or heartbeat, not needing the extra attention of authorities. He wasn't happy to remove the IV of morphine, but with his legs under him and leather straps removed, he could make a plan.

"Well, Doc. You wouldn't let us handcuff him, so I'm inclined to check in occasionally to make sure the patient is secure until he can be brought into custody," someone sternly said in the hallway in front of Ron's door.

So much for a plan, Ron thought as he moved as fast as he could with still-adjusting legs to the frame of the door. *I hope I only have to ruin one person's day.*

A policeman entered. But before he could call for help, Ron gave him a non-lethal blow to his windpipe and eased the door shut. Gasping for air, the officer was slowly lowered to the ground before a fist quickly connected with his temple to knock him out.

Ron switched from his peach-colored hospital gown and into the police uniform as fast as he could, keeping the badge. The uniform was slightly smaller in size than was comfortable, but it did the job. He put a pillow under the cop's head before taking his car keys, his Glock 9 mm semiautomatic handgun, and $150 cash from his wallet. He pulled the uniform cap down on his slightly larger head after transferring the oxygen and heart monitor to the officer.

Ron walked as subtly and casually as he could to the stairs and out of the hospital. It didn't take long before the building sounded alarms to staff and police. He had enough time to beep the locks on the set of car keys and find his victim's squad car. He started the car and fled two minutes before two other police cars converged on Woolrich Memorial Hospital.

- - - - -

Ron made a left turn with the squad car, having located Carey Sullivan's address with the on-board computer. He decided against making any trouble for his Aunt Peggy. He could only hope for the kindness of a co-worker who had saved his life. He had to admit to himself that his interest in her was less than practical.

What he saw at her address made his stomach churn. Her small rental unit had been burned to the ground. Police tape surrounded the charred remains of what had been Carey's home. He hoped the gal would've stayed away from her home after she bludgeoned a curly-haired jerk to save his worthless life. He needed to go somewhere and think.

Ron shrugged off thoughts of fleeing. Although he didn't have any love for his city, the one person he did love was nearby. He was also far too stubborn to leave a dangerous element that struck him first.

I'm gonna kick somebody's ass, good sense and self-preservation be damned, he thought. *I gotta get some nourishment first. Beer helps me think, after all, even more than morphine.*

There had to be somewhere where he could get some fried food and a beer to clear himself out of the liquid vitamins and other garbage Woolrich Memorial Hospital staff had fed to him. He remembered the Hooters in town and sighed.

"Not my first choice, but it'll have to do," he muttered to himself. "The first thing I gotta do is fit in better."

He headed to the town Walmart and ditched the squad car a good ways away after wiping down the computer, steering wheel, turn signal, shifter, and door handle for prints. After he walked to the superstore to "save money and live better," he picked up a pair of brown corduroys, a light blue button-down, a black windbreaker, and a White Sox baseball cap.

He then walked a mile and a half toward the Woolrich Hooters for beer, a burger, and some wings. There was enough room in the windbreaker to make the Glock unnoticeable in his chest pocket. He didn't think anyone at Hooters would be interested in his chest anyway.

Someone to Call a "Friend"

Carey Sullivan swabbed a table where a Hooters customer had just expelled the contents of his stomach after washing down a poorly-cooked chicken sandwich with a few Budweisers. The mess put her in a foul mood. Another surprise in the "Delightfully Tacky" chain restaurant of low-cut tops and low-cost thrills didn't improve her disposition.

The same asshole who got me into this mess just ordered from the hostess at one of my tables, Carey thought. *Might as well keep shoveling more good tidings onto this shit show.*

Sal Paretti had promptly let her go after she had smacked her shoe against the curly haired creep with the Beretta handgun. Paretti's official rationale was that she and the bouncers were too aggressive. Before getting into her Toyota Corolla, she phoned her friend, Lizzy, to see if she could hole up on her couch for a day or two.

Lizzy loved her son, John, so there was no issue about him staying for the near future. Carey was more than grateful to be put up for a day. It turned out it was a good thing she could stay at her friends; she learned the next morning that her apartment had burned the ground in a so-called accident.

Since she didn't want to endanger her friends or make it more difficult to watch over John, Carey rented a five hundred square foot studio apartment across from the Walmart. It was home until she felt safer.

Now some more trouble has to wander into my life, she thought, looking at Ron. She brought his Miller Lite and wings toward his table and gave a cold, but consciously cordial grin

"Ma'am, I would like the Double-D burger with all the fixings," he said. His widened eyes upon seeing her showed surprise.

"What the hell are you doing here?" Carey said in a barely subdued voice. "If you aren't on a deathbed, the cops are surely looking for you. Not to mention that some asshole burned down my place, with likely thanks to me helping out some street rat and my co-worker in the same day. I got no more time for charity cases. The burger will be $10. I'll add it onto your tab."

She scowled at the lines and furrowed eyebrows on his seemingly sorrow-filled face. He took off his White Sox cap.

"You don't take shit from anyone," he said in a soft voice, "I appreciate you saving my ass. I saw the number they did on your home. I can only give you this little extra for your troubles, for now. I wouldn't tell anyone where you got it."

Ron handed her a $50 bill and averted his eyes as she stuffed it in her cleavage and walked away. Carey could almost feel his eyes lingering on her. She brought him his food in about fifteen minutes and gave compulsory customer service, thanking him for his "robust generosity."

As he sipped his beer, she served her other customers. She showed them more warmth than the general act she gave him. After he was done and she cleared his plate, Ron had the nerve to ask when she was done with her shift to talk.

"I'll allow customers to have fantasies when I'm on the clock, but they can't butt in afterward," she said before handing him a receipt for food and the beer. "Why don't you show yourself out after you've paid up?"

- - - - -

While Ron considered the facts that he wasn't yet dead, in prison, or permanently disabled, he still found his situation pretty piss poor. Not only was he wanted by the police for getting shot while doing his job and defending himself, he had battered an officer and stole his squad car to evade authorities and other thugs. To boot, the cute stripper who saved his life and used to be friendly was now angry.

She's being pretty harsh, he thought. *I can't really blame her for being pissed, but is working at one shithole really worse than taking off your clothes at another shithole. I guess there is that whole house burning thing. But I didn't make you stick up for me. Also, those wings really sucked.*

Since he had nowhere to go and no clear plan in sight, he left Hooters and decided to walk the mile and a half back toward the Walmart. He decided to do some reconnaissance on the building where he had been renting a studio apartment.

Ron felt it would be nice if he didn't have to screw anyone else over for cash; the amount from his strong-arm robbery of the police officer was running thin. He could have used another beer, but he realized the walk was better.

Now that the pounding in my head is done and the squirrels who caused it are drunk, he thought, *I gotta stay alert.*

He didn't see any cops or other thugs who were looking for trouble in his apartment lot. He figured his studio had already been ransacked and rented out again. The sight of a police squad car in the Walmart lot put him on edge.

Ron crept to the Walmart, as hidden as he could from any authorities, to buy a lighter, a clearance sleeping bag, and some granola bars. He helped himself to extra large shopping bags for waterproofing his sleeping arrangements if it came to that. He decided to head back to the slightly more wooded area behind Hooters to camp out for the night. He was nearly out of cash and thought he could at least rip off someone who was drunk before the jerk tried to get in his car and possibly kill anyone while driving.

I'd like to try and have some honor, even though I'm a fugitive thief, he thought. *I just hope I'll get to see Aunt Peggy while she's still around. It's a good thing she believes in me and likely thinks that any official story is bullshit.*

- - - - -

Carey Sullivan was done around midnight at Hooters, finally able to change into a purple cotton tank top and some curve-hugging, black yoga pants. She said goodbye to the other waitresses and started walking across the parking lot to her used, rusty Toyota Corolla. She stopped when she saw the newer Lincoln parked two spots away.

Why would anyone who owned a Lincoln go to Hooters, or park near my tetanus trap on wheels? she thought. Two well-muscled arms soon grabbed her from behind.

Carey's self-defense training kicked in as she thrust her hips backward to throw her attacker off balance. She heard a deep grunt after she brought down her right heel on the attackers toe. She figured correctly that her swift kick to his groin would negate any power steroids could give him.

As her ski-masked assailant gasped for breath, a stocky, swarthy goon stepped out of the driver's side of the Lincoln and raised a handgun. She used the moment before she was in the gun's sights to give a kick to knock out the dope with the ski-mask. Her hands then flew up and she stared at the gun with eyes widened more out of defiance than fear.

"You try to kick *mi coglioni*, it won't do anything to dissuade a hole in your head," the handgun-wielding goon said. "So drop the tough stuff, *puttana*."

In an admittedly dark and malevolent way, Carey smiled after her captor was silenced by a loud gunshot from the nearby woods. Two other tough guys leapt out of the Lincoln back seat only for one to be shot in the kneecap, the other in the shoulder. Reacting on an instinct that so often served her well, she sprinted to them and knocked them each out with quick kicks to their respective temples.

The smirk on her face dissipated when she discovered that the guy who assisted her was the same jerk she blamed for her situation. She didn't bother taking the time to argue as she joined Ron in loading all the bodies, one dead and three injured, into the back seat of the Lincoln. To his credit, he did hold the door for her as she took the front passenger's seat. He also drove away before her manager could come out and see the carnage.

Despite all the trouble this buster's brought me, he does seem to have something going on between those ears, she thought as they drove along the back roads. *He at least seems to be in a decent mood for a change.*

The Lincoln sped on.

7

A Nice Place to Convalesce

Ron McCallister dropped the three injured brutes and one dead one near the mansion where Mayor George De Silva had lived with his viciously vapid children and woeful wife. He relieved the incompetent goons of over $500 that they collectively held in their wallets. The four also provided him with another Glock semiautomatic and more 9 mm ammo, a clip apiece. As he drove with Carey in the Lincoln, he felt good about being able to buy a few days without having to steal from anyone who didn't have it coming.

"Do you have any idea who wants us dead?" he asked. "Assholes are surprisingly abundant, even for this town. Anyone look familiar?"

"I think tonight has brought more conversation than we've had since you started at Starlet's Alley," Carey said. "Why are you so talkative all the sudden?"

"I like to talk when I'm in survival mode." he said. "I get focused when shit's on the line. You saved my life and you're attractive. Why not get to know you better?"

He figured the bright look in Carey's hazel eyes were from surprise or a sense of strength from seeing him blush. As heat seeped from his neck to behind his ears and into his cheeks, he beckoned her to talk by raising his right hand off the steering wheel. She mercifully took the hint.

Carey filled him in about the run-in with the late mayor's daughter and about the "olive-skinned assholes" who took the kid away in the Mustang. The two thugs were the same ones who caused trouble that last night at Starlet's alley. She also informed Ron that he was wanted for the murders of said thugs even though she remembered that one of them had left after shooting the other in the head.

"Hey, I admit I'm an asshole," he said. "But I don't kill anyone unless there isn't a choice. And with those morons, I had a choice."

"But not with the gunman tonight?" she asked.

"Well, you did save my ass, and it was either him or you," Ron said. "I figured I'd return the favor. I didn't see why some goon should pull a gun on a waitress, and I didn't kill the other three."

He scratched his chin before continuing.

"By the way, since we seem to be hunted by the same hitmen, we could check in with each other and help each other out. Intelligence sharing could be useful."

Ron watched as Carey stretched her legs in the passenger's seat. Her face grew serious as she tucked a stray lock of dark red hair behind her ear. He could tell she enjoyed the power she had over him and most men, and probably some women too.

"Since you helped get me into this mess, it'd be nice to have another helpful hand," she said a minute after adjusting the strap on her top. "I have a friend who still has a veneer of legitimacy. She's helping me by keeping an eye on my son. I also wouldn't mind collaborating with someone outside of the law; we'll have to bend to rules to stay alive."

He nodded ascent after admiring her fetching figure and attitude. As they headed back to the Hooters, she drifted to unconsciousness while he drove. He felt good that someone who wasn't family put some trust in him.

Why do I only find the will to do what's right and meet a nice girl when shit hits the fan? he thought. *I better just keep my eyes on the road and make sure this gal stays safe.*

He drove in silence while keeping himself occupied on thoughts of hitmen, the late Mayor De Silva, and corruption in Woolrich. It was easier to focus on that than deal with his fascination with Carey and other tendencies toward vulnerability.

- - - - -

The second time she arrived at Hooters in 24 hours, a gentle nudge to the shoulder awoke Carey before she had to make the conscious decision to unfasten her seat belt, open the door, and step out of the Lincoln. She wandered toward her Toyota Corolla with sleep clouding her coordination. She knew that she could drive home, but decided that the oaf who had helped her out tonight would probably be more safe on the roads. He had given her $250 of the looted funds from her would-be assassins.

I trust him enough to drive me around while I take a nap, she thought. *Would it hurt to offer him shelter for the night?*

"You need a place to stay?" she asked after making a few steps to return toward the Lincoln. "I rent a studio apartment across from the Walmart where you could hole up for a while. I registered it using fake ID I still have from when I was 19. Still works."

He grimaced and rocked from foot to foot while she asked. She found it cute.

"I was going to dump the Lincoln at St. Francis," he said. "If you follow, we could take your Toyota to your place. I'd appreciate a day or two there to play it safe"

Carey followed as he drove to the Catholic church to drop off the Lincoln. He then drove her Toyota back to her apartment. He gently woke her again when they got to her parking lot.

Ron followed her up the steps to her second floor studio apartment. She sensed that he was admiring her legs and told him to watch his step. After she let him in, he rolled his sleeping bag a few feet away from her twin-sized mattress. He actually asked if it was okay that he slept on the floor near her.

She gave him a sleepy smile and a nod before she offered generic Tylenol PM. They both took a dose before falling into a wonderful, restorative slumber. Carey awoke to the smell of cheese, bacon, and eggs frying in her kitchen.

I could get used to this, she thought. *Ron can stay a while longer if he keeps this up.*

8

Violence, Sensuality, and a Decent Breakfast

The Sicilian collected his three living but roughed up tough guys just before dawn in front of the mansion where the De Silvas used to live. The fourth had a gunshot to the head that created even more unwanted attention. He had to pay off the press and the police so that they wouldn't ask more questions than required of them.

How hard is it to knock off a recently-hired waitress outside of a Hooters? the Sicilian thought. *The money I was going to pay these four will go toward bribes. Several hundred dollar bills should help the coppers pay less mind.*

A well-compensated policeman reminded the Sicilian that Ron McCallister was still at large. A loud four-letter word formed in the Sicilian's head in response to the obvious. He would've killed the officer out of spite if it wouldn't have garnered national attention to the area. There were some things that he couldn't hide with hush money if he lost his temper.

The first thing he had to to do was find out if his three living, wanna-be hitmen knew anything. They failed with a simple task. Obviously, if they were still alive, whoever took them out of commission had a bigger conscience than he had. He looked forward to releasing some steam back at his greystone.

Frankie, who had taken a kick to his nuts but no gun shot wounds, was the first to go after he explained his side of the story. He got beaten up by a woman, a sexpot who'd recently had a career change. This was a lethal disgrace. The Sicilian shot two rounds from his Ruger into the thug's forehead.

The other two spoke about a gunshot from the darkness. They didn't even get a description of their assailant before Carey knocked them unconscious. One of them offered the idea of being thwarted by "the bitch's guardian angel." The boss seemed to find this funny. At least he was the only one laughing when the Associate carved "Hooters" into their foreheads before slicing their femoral arteries. The screaming quieted within minutes.

The Sicilian had more than a hunch that Ron McCallister was helping out Carey. A *Naperville Sun* article had mentioned McCallister's "disappearance" the night before from Woolrich Memorial Hospital. A police officer found in his room didn't remember any details.

The Sicilian planned on a visit to his competition in the local sphere of influence, a certain Sal Paretti. The owner of Starlet's Alley would also likely be interested in the happenings of his former employees. Paretti probably wouldn't do what was necessary to stop loose ends, but the Sicilian could use some leverage for a deal on Woolrich real estate.

"These Micks are becoming a thorn in my side," the Sicilian grumbled to the Associate. "We gotta take them out to get the upper hand on Paretti. Then the mob and me can cash in on the suburban rackets."

The Associate nodded before washing off the knife and snorting cocaine, which was Woolrich's main export. It was still relatively early in the day, and a chemical rush helped bring the world into focus.

- - - - -

Generic instant granules were the only way to make so-called coffee at Carey Sullivan's apartment. So before she woke up, Ron took a short trip to Walmart to pick up a French press, bacon, eggs, and cheese, Great Value Espresso, a *Sun-times*, and Just For Men hair coloring. He was already mostly gray at 30 years of age. The gray didn't bother him, but changing his appearance to look somewhat younger was a welcome step to evade prison or death. He waited to do it until his new roommate had awoken.

Ron quietly washed the pans in the sink after admiring the dark red waves on Carey's head, poking up with disarray over her covers. His admiration for the outline of her curvy behind and muscular legs under the simple light blue quilt confirmed his fears. The gal was getting under his skin. He hadn't felt that way for a while, which was a mixture of pleasant excitement and discomfort. While cleaning her dishes, he realized that he was going into into unfamiliar territory.

Maybe it's the fact that she's sexy yet still resourceful and can kick the crap out of greaseballs, he thought. *I'm not just cleaning to be nice to a pretty gal. I really can't stand a dirty kitchen.*

Ron didn't worry as much about waking her when he dropped the eggs, cheese, and bacon in the hand-me-down frying pan on her built-in stove top. It was almost ten by that point. He could see her stirring as water boiled in a small sauce pan so that he could press the coffee. Carey had no real dishes in the cabinets. He only found Hooters to-go boxes and Styrofoam cups to serve breakfast on a small card table.

She actually smiled at him as she reached her arms above her head and stretched her legs from under an oversize t-shirt that dropped to mid-thigh. He was somewhat nervous when she put on some wool socks lying by her mattress and padded over to him. Twelve hours ago, he expected a slap across the face. Instead, she gave him a flirty kiss on the cheek before disappearing in the small bathroom. The small wrinkles at the outside edges of her hazel eyes somehow made her look sexier.

"Holy shit," he muttered to himself as he realized that his piqued interest was visible below the waist.

He splashed some cold water on his face from the small kitchenette faucet before he finished cooking breakfast and went to sit down at the table. He tried to calm down with the *Sun-Times* while she was in the bathroom. All the stories on Woolrich's missing "murdering bouncer" didn't help him relax. What interested him was that the fallout from last night's ruckus at Hooters hadn't received much more coverage than a police brief. There also wasn't even mention of four thugs, one whom was very dead outside of the former mayor's mansion.

Although he rarely read the business section, something caught his eye on the front page. Apparently, Nicholas Ferranti, an alleged mob guy from Chicago, was interested in expanding and buying an entertainment venue in Woolrich. The potential seller was one Salvatore Paretti. Ron figured he'd have to find out more. There was more to the story that would shed light on problems for him and Carey.

He put down the paper as Carey came back

to the living area about ten minutes after she had kissed him. Her milky skin was freshly washed and her red locks were pinned up in a clip. She wore a simple, white terry cloth robe and sat down at the card table before crossing her legs.

"It smells wonderful in here," she said with a smile. "What are we having?"

- - - - -

Carey Sullivan showed her company that even though she could clean up and make anyone stand at attention with her beauty, she had an appetite, manners be damned. She scarfed down her eggs and bacon and wiped her mouth with her sleeve. Ron used a disposable Hooters napkin to pick at a stain on the table after eating the eggs.

As he poured them both French-pressed coffee to finish the meal, she got up and found the non-dairy, sweetened creamer from a high cupboard. She knew he was likely checking out her behind as she stood on her tip-toes to make the reach. He declined the creamer with a slight shake of his head as she dumped a few teaspoons in hers.

"You're pretty polite for the hardened thug that the news keeps referring to. The fact that you not only haven't made a drunken proposition to me, but cleaned my so-called kitchen and made me scrumptious eggs makes me wonder. Where'd you learned to be such a capable, conscientious man around the house."

"Spent some time in the Army when we went to 'liberate' Iraq five years ago," he said. "I did a lot of mess duty since I didn't like taking orders. I usually didn't get along with my CO. Even so, I kept to the mission and learned how to fight and keep things squared away before I finished my requisite tours. I'm not sure if that made me a good guy."

Carey giggled before responding.

"Well, I meant to imply that you don't act like a jerk, not necessarily that you were a good guy. By the way, most guys who consider themselves 'good guys' are full of shit. I'm happier that you simply know how to cook and not be a pervert. At least I wouldn't be scared to let you near my son if I try to see him in the next few days."

She noticed the way Ron blushed. She interrupted with an attempt at humor:

"Yeah, most guys might consider me a MILF," she teased. "I've noticed your glances. It's my physical assets that help me pay the bills."

She finished a slice of bacon before interrupting an awkward silence.

"Seriously, before yesterday I thought you were either gay or an asshole."

"Well, now that we're getting personal, you may be the second closest person to this asshole at the moment," he said after a chuckle. "There is one lady who is my rock. She stepped in when my biological father didn't do his job."

They stared at each other a bit in silence before he retrieved the French press to top off their coffee.

"If the Army taught you cleaning, killing, and discipline, this lady must have taught you cooking and good manners." Carey said. "Tell me about her."

In as few a words as possible, Ron talked about how Aunt Peggy was the one who saved him from Dad's temper by threatening to shoot him if he laid down more beatings. She was the one who told him to stick to school and get a

Bachelor's Degree from Loyola University in Criminal Justice. This led to the Army because he couldn't find a job and needed to pay off loans.

"How'd you get to be a bouncer at Starlet's Alley?" she pressed.

"After Iraq, I came back to Chicago, got kicked out of police academy, worked construction, and finally ended up at a strip club. When Aunt Peggy got sick, I wanted to be closer to her and get paid to be a hard-ass."

"Sounds like a heck of ride. I wish I'd gotten to know you better before shit hit the fan. The mutual need to stay alive isn't necessary to be social."

"It helps for me," he said with a grin.

She excused herself from the table after a sip from her coffee and an adjustment to her robe to close the widening gap of her neckline. She had a feeling that Ron was opening up to her, but she remembered that she had to call Lizzy before work if she wanted to hear about her son. She took out her Motorola Razr and dialed.

"Carey, where the hell have you been?" Lizzy asked her over the phone. "WGN news said the police are searching for a bouncer you used to work with and that the press is unable to find you for comment. Are you alone? Do you want me to come and get you? Do you need any help, honey?"

"Lizzy, please don't worry about me. If you look after my son, I can look after myself," Carey said. "As for the missing bouncer, he just cooked us both breakfast and was chatting with me about family. If he keeps on being kind and not being a homicidal maniac, I'd like to introduce him to John. What do you think?"

"You're hanging out with the killer bouncer?"

Lizzy said. "Have you gone off your rocker?!"

"Lizzy, I'm fine," Carey said. "I love you and what you're doing for John. I don't know how I'll ever pay you back for taking care of him. Just pretend that he's bunking over at Brian's for awhile. I'll help you somehow when I get situated. You know I will."

"He and my Brian are watching Toy Story for the second time today," Lizzy said. "The kids are having a good time, but John still asks for Mommy."

"When you give him a glass of warmed milk, have yourself some Southern Comfort. It'll calm you down some," Carey said. "Tell him I'm on a business trip and I'll see him when I get back soon. I'll try to check-in regularly. I love you, dear"

"You take care of yourself, hon."

"I will if you do."

When Carey flipped her phone to end the call, she noticed that Ron had cleaned her pans and taken out the trash.

"Would you mind if I used your shower?" he asked. "I am smelling pretty ripe and I don't just like clean kitchens. Also, I need to change my hair color from gray to black. I think I'll grow my beard for awhile. Try not to freak out if a dark-haired, scruffy man comes out."

Carey gave him a warm smile and nodded before responding.

"Well, you better hurry up because I still gotta get to work, flashing my cleavage and selling burgers," she said. "By the way, I think black hair will suit you well. Trim beards are kinda sexy."

She enjoyed the blush in his smirking cheeks before he went to get cleaned up. She finished her coffee and got dressed in her Hooters uniform by the time he came back out. She gave him a nod of approval before entering the bathroom to apply lipstick and mascara.

"My shift ends at ten tonight. You can come back here if you need to spend the night," Carey after she applied her makeup. "Until then, try not to draw attention to your new look by roughing up too many people, handsome."

He just nodded politely before they left her apartment and went separate ways.

9

Strip Joints and Public Libraries

Starlet's Alley was buzzing with fluorescent lighting, fake smiles, fake breasts, and a restocked bar before the Sicilian entered in the late afternoon and ordered a Perrier. It arrived at a private booth before he sat down. He asked a bikini-clad waitress to send Sal Paretti to his table with a bottle of Glenlivet and two snifters.

Paretti brought the Scotch and snifters to the booth with slumped shoulders and shifty eyes. He hesitantly took the seat across from the Sicilian. He poured them each a few fingers of the Speyside whisky. The booze was, of course, on the house.

"I was thinking that we made you a hell of an offer on this shithole," the Sicilian said in Italian. "I'm wondering why in the devil's name you refused it."

Paretti wiped the sweat off his brow and scratched his throat with the back of his hand. He was supposed to be more relaxed since he recently armed his guards with Glock semiautomatic handguns. He would feel better, however, if they had assault rifles. He realized that the only way he could take the advantage in a rigged game was to show off the size of his *coglioni*.

"I've gotta hunch that you had something to do with the death of my pal, the late Mayor George De Silva," he said in the same tongue in which he was addressed. "The fill-in mayor, Rob Peck, likely has the same hunch. The thing is, I've got local connections and intel that you don't have. And while you may have a more established brand and more connections on a state and national level, you gotta work with the locals."

The Sicilian's eyes widened, but he stayed calm. He began picking under his fingernails. He tried to appear as if he was stifling a yawn.

"Look at the big local businessman with mob ties throwing his almost three hundred pounds around," he responded in an even voice. "The thing is, I could pay hit men less than any offer we gave for this shithole. For that lower amount, I could take out you, the rest of De Silva's family, your new mayor, his wife, and his one child. I think this Peck guy will be more copacetic than De Silva, so me and the family would like to offer payoff to you and him. Too much violence isn't good for business. What the hell is your problem, Sal? You don't like money?"

Paretti adjusted his collar and nodded at his armed bouncer before answering.

"The thing is," he said with a firmness that slightly surprised the Sicilian, "I built this business and have a staff that would gladly make sure that you never have an honest orgasm or straight piss the rest of your life. Since this is my place, you'll have to take out my armed gunmen right now before you get a shot at me. This is my home and my livelihood."

The Sicilian adjusted his tie and poured himself a double of the Scotch before doing the same for Paretti. He picked at a right incisor with the end of his tongue before calmly responding.

"I've underestimated you," he said. "I mostly do that when I'm dealing with the darkies and Polaks in Chicago. But if you want to play hardball, it doesn't matter how tough you think you are. It depends on how many higher-ups are willing to support you with guns and cash."

"Short-term or long-term?" Paretti asked before he snapped his fingers and two bouncers came to his side and revealed their Glocks. "I don't care that you come from a long line of Mafioso. Al Capone's descendants and I play golf when they make it to the burbs."

The Sicilian chuckled as he put the palms of his hands on the table. He nodded and the two bouncers got knocked in the heads by two gorillas in polo shirts who had been playing it cool at the bar. Their boss stuck a switchblade in the table as he got up. One of the thugs collected the bottle of Glenlivet. The other dusted off a fedora and placed it on the Sicilian's head before motioning to the automatic handgun in his belt.

Paretti signaled for other bouncers to stand down.

"You should be nicer to your customers, Paretti," the Sicilian said. "I don't know how you'll stay in business for very long if you keep threatening those who want to offer you a healthy severance package for a joint full of strippers. I know they're a front, and that the real money comes from stuff DEA acquaintances of mine would be interested in finding. But what good is money if you have to lose your freedom or your life?"

After the Sicilian left with the bottle of Scotch and his two musclebound helpers, Paretti went to his office in the back of the club and sulked. The only way to put him in the right mood to get through the rest of the night was to partake his own product. The cocaine did a better job of keeping his customers hooked than the booze, breasts, behinds, and charming decor.

Two bouncers, whom the Sicilian's goons had knocked out, found Paretti an hour later and revived him. Under his bloody nose, a thin sheen of white powder remained on his upper lip. He promptly wiped it off with his handkerchief and took a shot from a fifth of Canadian Club hidden in his desk. He and the bouncers had to join other employees to keep an eye on the dance floor, the bar, and the space where spectators drank in booze and visions of flesh.

It was still relatively early in the evening and Paretti had to keep customers entertained in his strip club. He reassured himself that the Sicilian would never be able to run things as smoothly. He was the only one who knew which strippers were preferred by certain local legislators, the DuPage County commissioner, and so-called local business elites.

- - - - -

Ron took the Metra train to Naperville to visit the Nichols Branch of the public library. Woolrich didn't bother with public schools or access to information. The forty or so school-age kids in the town were happy to get out of town for an education at public schools in the nearby suburbs of Naperville or Lisle. Ron didn't blame them.

Once he accessed ProQuest databases using his account at the Nichols Branch, he researched all relevant local and national media for the terms "Ferranti, Salvatore Paretti, and Starlet's Alley." Having not much luck, he searched again for "Ferranti, Paretti" and he replaced "Starlet's Alley" with "local business." He limited the search results to the past six months.

This new ProQuest search showed a number of hits connecting his three search terms, one of

which stuck out in his mind. A gossip columnist
for the *Naperville Sun* wrote that Nicholas
Ferranti's "alleged connection to the Chicago
mob will help him negotiate for a larger cut in
the alleged sale of narcotics from a local
Woolrich business." The business turned out to
be owned by an S. Paretti.

Public court records showed tax-evasion and
racketeering charges for Ferranti, with acquittals
for murder and the possession and sale of
narcotics. A *Sun-Times* clip corresponding to the
murder case cited "a lack of witnesses and
material evidence." Ron began his focus on
Nicholas Ferranti as a person of interest that
either police were either too oblivious or too
well-compensated to investigate.

*Is Ferranti calling all the shots himself? How
deep is he connected with local politicians and
police?* he thought during his search.

Ron shut down his search and logged out of
his computer when he saw police officers
questioning one of the library clerks. He knew
that the clerk had a professional duty to not
monitor the research and other inquiries of
patrons.

*Thank goodness library workers hate the
Patriot Act as much as I do,* he thought.

Law enforcement could still query about
those who posed a threat to so-called national
security.

*Unemployed, former strip club bouncers are a
big threat,* he thought as he went out the door of
the Nichols Branch. *I only killed one person in
my life while not in the Army, and that was to
protect Carey. Won't the defense just rest on
that? Everyone likes a sexy former stripper,
especially one with a brain.*

Ron got on a Metra train and rode back to Woolrich, wishing he could visit his Aunt Peggy without getting her involved in this garbage. He also longed for a few gulps of Evan Williams bourbon, but he couldn't afford such an indulgence at the moment.

He wondered if his former boss could lend some credence to his suspicions. He decided to don his White Sox cap and pay a visit to Paretti. No one was interested in scruffy guys in caps at a strip club.

- - - - -

Sal Paretti watched a muscular man in a black t-shirt and a White Sox cap enter the club later that evening as the cocaine and whisky began to wear off. He thought the man looked familiar in a way, but rationalized that he was probably some asshole millennial from the burbs who thought it was cool to mimic people from the more working-class, South Side Chicago. He thought he'd have a little fun with the poseur.

I can hold my own against hostile goombahs from the Chicago mob, he thought. *How hard could this dipshit be?*

Paretti sent the two bouncers who had revived him a few hours earlier to give some grief to the asshole. However, both of them walked briskly away from the man in the Sox cap and back to their boss.

"He says he wants to talk to management," a crew cut-styled, musclebound bouncer told him. "Sounds pretty urgent, boss."

"Tell him that if he doesn't order a drink soon, he'll urgently be kicked out of here on his stupid ass."

The tough guy with the crew-cut seemed genial when he went back to the man with the cap, as if the customer was the one signing his paychecks. The man then ordered a club soda and lime. The bouncer served him with a deferential grin.

Who is this shithead? thought Paretti. *Would he take the job as a bouncer? If he can make my current bouncers wet their pants, he'd likely be better in a fight against that Sicilian joker. What's with the candy ass club soda?*

"How you like the view?" he asked him after approaching. He noticed the visitor had pulled down the brim of hat and didn't make eye contact as they shook hands.

What if he was clean-shaven? Paretti thought.

"I'd appreciate it if there was more male talent." the cryptic customer said. "The Boystown neighborhood in the city is more my scene for eye candy. But since I moved in with my boyfriend in the burbs, I'm looking more for nose candy. Will that still be coming in?"

"Congratulations, you're a fag." Paretti deadpanned, turning to the stage and the busty brunette dancing there. "As for candy, not sure what you mean by nose candy. We officially have a 'look but don't touch' policy with the gals during business hours. You'd be hard-pressed to get a taste of that sweet stuff even if you weren't a queer."

Paretti made an effort not to look at the man with the Sox cap. He didn't want any gays to get the wrong idea, after all.

"I guess I shouldn't believe gossipers. Although, I was wondering if this joint is still hiring bouncers after the staff issues some days ago. If so, my man is interested. He's really strong and you'd have no problems between him and your talent. He's also willing to win over anyone if there's a change in ownership. Or is that gossip too?"

Maybe it's the cocaine talking, maybe it's the nancy in my club, but I'm starting to freak out, Paretti thought as he started to wipe his nose.

"We ain't hiring. Got enough muscled gorillas as it stands." he said as blood started dripping down a nostril. "You queers oughta stay away from my club, at any rate. I got an itchy trigger finger and a low tolerance for dudes who like dudes."

Paretti didn't excuse himself before he fled into his back office.

- - - - -

Ron McCallister had seen guys crash from a coke high a couple times in college and in the Army. He could spot from across the room that Paretti was using. To get to him, he just flashed the stolen police badge briefly to the hired goons and told them he was looking more to buy candy than to make a bust.

Fortunately for him, the inept bouncers didn't pay him more attention after he prodded Paretti for information. The one with with the crew cut had muscles but lacked a brain.

No sign of the bouncer who was quick with the phone and the gun to help Carey and I, Ron thought. *He must have been too competent to keep on staff. That's some relief for a fugitive.*

Paretti's reaction to Ron's false identity as a gay man successfully kept his former boss at a distance. Ron congratulated himself on playing on prejudices that he didn't have personally.

What two or more consenting guys or gals do in the bedroom is none of my damned business, Ron thought. *It's funny that so many "freedom-loving" politicians are interested in the private bedroom goings-on between adults.*

From his observation and library research, Ron suspected that Paretti and Ferranti were negotiating the sale of Starlet's Alley to mask the mob's incursion into cocaine in the western suburbs. He didn't have any definitive evidence about who was in charge of all the death threats and media attention against both him and Carey.

Just as he received his second drink, a ginger ale on the rocks, an unfamiliar bartender told him that he had a call. The investigation had to wait.

- - - - -

Carey Sullivan stood by the phone in the staff room at the end of her shift. She still wore her low-cut Hooters tank top while she thought about where her new roommate could be. She decided to give their former employer an anonymous call.

"I knew you weren't still on the payroll there, but I had a hunch that you might be casing the joint to find out what's going on," she said after Ron took the phone from the bartender. "I just described your scruffy looks and your White Sox cap to the barman. I was lecherous enough to get him to hurry."

"It's almost too bad that I'm not on the payroll here," Ron told her. "They could really use a competent bouncer. I have a story to tell you that may illuminate how our fortunes play out. You should pick me down the street from Starlet's Alley to hear about my fun-filled day at the library and later at a less sexy place."

"On my way, tough guy," she said after a snort to show her amusement.

Carey drove her Corolla a ways down the street from Starlet's Alley and picked him up.

When they got back to her apartment, she shed her clothes in the bathroom before emerging with the t-shirt that fell just above mid-thigh. He entered the bathroom and did the hygiene required of him before emerging. He started to make his bed on the floor.

"Come here for a minute," she said, patting her twin mattress. "You have to tell me what you've found out while I've been busy working my physical assets."

Ron coyly took a seat and then told her about what he had found at the public library. He filled her in on his own conclusions after seeing their old boss. The connection between Ferranti and Paretti seemed to make sense, even if evidence was circumstantial. He grew quiet before he asked her something she couldn't help but oblige.

"My Aunt Peggy is dying in a Naperville hospice," he said. "She's wanted to see me with a cute gal since I hit seventeen. She means the world to me, and I wondered if you could make the trip while I'm in limbo. I know we've just barely gotten to know each other, but she needs to feel that her nephew is branching out."

"Well, from your stories, she sounds like a pistol," she said. "Tell you what, I'll do it if you make me breakfast tomorrow. Will next Monday work? It's one of my days off."

"I'll call ahead and tell her," he said, with a huge smile on his face.

"Your ability to cook and play detective makes me think that I'll be able to be with my son sooner rather than later," she said. "Why don't you get a better night's rest and join me on this deluxe twin mattress that came with my studio apartment?"

The rest of the night, Ron listened to her breath as he lay next to her. Unconsciously, she tried to spoon him at times. She didn't have much trouble sleeping in peace while searching for comfort, intimacy, or both. He spent two hours wondering what the hell he was doing before the need for shut-eye overtook him.

10

Trouble in Paradise

The blaze erupting near Starlet's Alley wasn't more than fifty yards from a trailer that served as Sal Paretti's home. Paretti woke up with his nose still bloody and his urine soiling his bed sheets. He put on a set of cleaner pants lying on the less soiled floor and wiped his nose on a hairy forearm before exiting.

Police and volunteer firefighters responded to the ensuing fire within two minutes. Shortly afterward, at around four a.m., an officer with a round face and a blond crew cut met with Paretti outside the trailer. He was chewing enough Skoal to make a mortician nauseous. The scent amplified Paretti's lingering nausea.

"Well, there's no immediate signs of arson around your trailer or your club, Mr. Paretti," the officer said before spitting a large brown wad to mix with the gravel on the ground. "The explosive fire resulted from a Ford Focus in your parking lot. We've got investigators looking at the cause, but I'd say it's likely an electrical problem or a corroded fuel line."

Paretti took in some air, trying not to vomit as shock and the effects of various chemicals conspicuously caught up to him.

"Oh, that's a sure as shit a relief...officer," he said, after a few coughs. "Sorry about the language, but I got woken up by a blast near my home and business. Was anyone in the car? I'm a sponsor for Designated Drivers of Illinois. So if someone has a few too many, I set them up with a ride to die on their own property."

"The only deceased was a person in the

driver's seat," the officer said. "We don't even know for sure whether the corpse is male or female. Hopefully, dental records will help us notify next-of-kin."

Paretti scratched his head and wiped his nose as the police officer tried to ask rudimentary questions. His spastic movements would have aroused suspicion if the officer cared to notice. Paretti eventually started hyperventilating and stopped responding, dropping to the ground as his eyes grew wide and glossy. His pupils shrunk to the size of pin pricks.

The officer called for the lone ambulance at the scene, which included two heavy, olive-skinned heavy guys and a more fair-skinned female. The officer thought she was a teenager at first glance. Even though he was suspicious, the officer was more prone to give emergency professionals the same deference he was afforded as one of Woolrich's finest.

Isn't Memorial Hospital the other way? he thought as he watched the ambulance drive away, spit more Skoal to the ground, and ran a hand through his blond crew cut. *I'd like to follow suspicious behavior, but the chief made it clear that I stay put to guard the perimeter. Checking on emergency staff won't mean any more pay for me. Screw it.*

- - - - -

The second in a number of pains that the Sicilian gave Paretti was a punch to his ample belly. The first involved a blow to where the club owner's doctor checks annually for a hernia. Paretti's labored breathing and scrunched face showed he was in a place of desperation. He didn't care anymore about his pride, his business, or even where to take his next pee. He was just hoping he wouldn't get any more shots to his sensitive areas. He was about to be disappointed.

"Tell me who controls this town. Who's got your balls in a vice? Who's gonna inherit illicit interests in this western Chicago suburb?" the Sicilian asked. "Who deserves the winning hand in the poker game that is Woolrich? Who owns the cocaine that comes into Chicago and wonderfully wrecks junkies of all stripes?"

"All that I want to do is make you happy, signore," Paretti said while laying on the grass by a secluded, pine-scented stretch of woods. "You deserve all the credit in how Woolrich develops. That stripper and those two bouncers who caused trouble the other night, I fired them. What else you want me to do?"

The Sicilian laughed in a deep voice when the Associate straddled Paretti. A mask disguised any identification as a thin line of powder ran under the concealed nose. Fear gripped Paretti as crazy yet familiar eyes looked back at him.

"I think my dedicated soldier here is bent on a coke rush," he said. "I can say that I appreciate your humility and telling us something we already well know. The trouble for you is that I can't talk down anyone who's just had some happy trails of candycaine."

The Associate produced a switchblade and jabbed it into Paretti's right shoulder, twisting clockwise as he screamed. The switchblade exited with a splash of blood and then was positioned in the air above the femoral artery in his left leg. The Sicilian shot the ground with his Ruger and everyone in the room fell silent, except for Paretti. He quickly quieted down his moans of agony to the best of his ability.

"The deal for you, Sal," the Sicilian said, "is that I can tend to your wounds in two minutes and make sure you don't feel pain until a not-yet-administered, nonlethal dose of morphine wears off if you promise me two things."

"Whatever you want me to do," Paretti promised. "It's done or you can kill my mother too, if you want."

The Sicilian wiped his face, took his Ruger, and shot Paretti where the switchblade had been a minute ago.

"Don't you ever disparage the name of your mother," he said. "I don't tolerate a son who speaks ill of his mother. You do that again, I'll slice off your *coglionis*. The first thing you need to do to stop feeling pain for the next twelve hours is agree to sign over the deed for Starlet's Alley to me with the very generous offer of $100,000. Second, you can't say anything to the authorities, reporters, or any gals-for-hire about me or my persuasive methods."

"Si, Signore," Paretti said before the Sicilian ordered a doctor with a revoked license to inject him with 75 milligrams of morphine. The mob medic stopped his bleeding, applied semi-sterile bandages, and administered smuggled antibiotics. He'd keep an eye on their charge until later that day.

11

Killer Fallout

Ron McCallister woke up at nine a.m. to the sound of Carey's heavy breathing. He turned on his side and admired the view as she as she did push-ups in a sports bra and what most guys describe as "booty shorts." He slid off of the twin mattress and started his first push-up beside her. He was happy to have a workout partner and didn't mind the view when she started sit-ups.

As he finished his own sit-ups, she went in to her small bathroom for a shower. When she was done, the towel wrapped around her red hair made him smile. He took a few seconds halfway through cooking breakfast to admire the curves just covered by her robe. She caught him glancing at her muscular legs and gave him a smirk.

He finished fixing the bacon and cheese omelets he was making for them as she returned to the steamy bathroom to slip into her Hooters uniform. She returned in five minutes to a card table set with two Styrofoam plates, two plastic forks, and two omelets. He poured her a fresh cup of coffee in a Styrofoam cup before returning to the stove top to fetch a some slightly singed wheat toast.

"Alright, cowboy," she said. "After eating, you need to get in there and wash up after your big workout. The scent of your cooking is amazing and I appreciate it more than you know. But it still doesn't hide your B.O."

So much for inflated egòs in front of a beautiful lady, he thought.

He ate slowly and lifted his arms frequently

just to taunt her before he went to shower. After ten minutes of a good soap and rinse, he enjoyed the grin on her face and cheeky wink of approval when he emerged fully-clothed and mostly clean-smelling.

"Much better," she said. "Since it's Friday and I could use a bit of family time, how would you like to meet my boy tonight? I switched shifts at Hooters from 11:30 until 8:00. I figure any more hitmen would be less likely to strike before ten p.m. Also my boss agrees that I'm the best server in the joint, so he'll give me flexibility."

"I'd be honored to meet your son," he said, "but I don't want to attract unwanted attention. I changed my hair color and have some facial hair, but it's still a flimsy disguise. How do you want to play this?"

Carey crossed her legs and her arms as her cheekbones grew tight. Her hazel eyes looked straight into his.

"I threw off some attention last night by taking a detour on the way to Starlet's Alley," she said. "I'm still looking for assholes who want to follow me until I'm helpless and alone. But I assure you, I'm not alone and I'm very rarely helpless."

Ron recognized passion and pride with traces of vulnerability. Even though he'd never personally found any connection to parenting, he assumed that it was a phenomena his Aunt Peggy showed. He could understand that.

"I'll help you and your son as long as I'm around," he said. "It's what my Aunt Peggy modeled for me in a way, and I feel it only right that I show the same courtesy to you."

"I hope you'll stick around a while longer, then," she said. "But you can only plan for the next day."

"No kidding," Ron said, "these mob thugs can really mess things up, at least for the short-term."

Carey kissed him on the cheek before she walked out the door, down the stairs, and to her rusty Toyota Corolla to start off to work. During the kiss, she handed him a key to her studio apartment.

"Meet me in the lot at Hooters at eight fifteen," she said in the doorway. "The less attention drawn to my digs or those of my girlfriend, the better. We might have to lose some thugs along the way."

He nodded in understanding as he watched her go. He then decided to catch up on the news before any more snooping around.

Ron walked to the Walmart to pick up a *Naperville Sun*, a package of black t-shirts, and a pair of gray cargo pants before he returned to Carey's studio and settled in for the next half hour with a few cups of coffee.

Aside from the latest gangland drama with Operation Family Secrets in Chicago, he read a three inch blurb in the police blotter about a car fire outside Starlet's Alley. Police didn't consider any foul play despite an unidentifiable corpse. This seemed odd to Ron. Any potential investigation wasn't likely far along.

In possibly related news, a larger article on the first page of the business section described how Starlet's Alley was likely to change owners. Nicholas Ferranti had gained confidence that Woolrich businessman, Salvatore Paretti, would "have to accept a less generous offer on his local business because of fluctuations in the economy."

I haven't noticed a decrease in clientele at Starlet's Alley, Hooters, or Walmart, he thought. *I should take a walk back over to the strip club and see what's going on in the wake of a car fire that officially wasn't suspicious. None of this makes sense.*

- - - - -

Among the many signs that something was amiss at Starlet's Alley, the one that stuck out the most to Ron was the carbon residue left from an explosive fire in one of the parking spaces near the front entrance. Police tape surrounded the spot where he remembered a Ford Focus had been the previous evening. It had struck him as odd then when he saw a strangely familiar man supposedly sleeping in the driver's seat of the Focus. Since he had been more interested in seeing Carey, he chose not to dwell on it. That might have been a mistake.

It was likely too early in the evening for some guy to drink himself toward slumber and pass out before starting his car, Ron thought before some latent details struck him. *The guy looked vaguely like the bouncer who called for police the night I got shot, only a little roughed up.*

Among the questions filling his head, Ron wondered if the driver of the Focus wasn't already dead. Ferranti's sudden optimism, according to the *Sun*, made him think that there were larger forces at play. Aside from the police tape around where the Focus had been parked, Ron noticed one squad car present at the end of the parking lot. He decided to try to find out more inside in club.

"Please take off your hat," said a bald-headed bouncer as he entered shortly after the club's four p.m. opening. "We've had some security concerns in the past couple of days."

Ron's trim beard and blackened hair made him feel comfortable enough to remove his Sox cap and keep a sharp eye out for Paretti. Despite the noticeable bulge in the bouncer's chest to suggest a firearm, he didn't notice any particular additional concern from among the dull muscle and barely less dull dancers on the stage. He didn't hold it against the dancers. His opinions about women, in general, had risen substantially after keeping house with Carey the last few days. Something other than a downturn in the economy must have shaken up Paretti to make him want to sell.

An explosion in his parking lot would do it, he thought. *Paretti never had a strong stomach for competition. It's possible that Nicholas Ferranti played a hand in the explosions and the change of fortunes. I hope the wait staff is chatty.*

"How is the owner of this joint, Salvatore Paretti?" Ron asked a blonde waitress in a pink tube top and silver miniskirt, the bottom of which ran to tan thighs. "I read that he's about to sell the joint. I applaud his willingness to promote business in Woolrich. If you get in with Chicago, you sell to the world, am I right?"

The waitress hadn't any idea what had happened to her boss, nor was she aware of the news surrounding her place of employment.

"I'm afraid the manager is not in, sir," she said. "He is currently attending to a personal family emergency."

"I hadn't heard about that," Ron said. "It's too bad that business success doesn't always translate to the personal realm. Please give him my best from Little Italy Syndicate Productions, won't you?"

"Sure thing, sir," she said. "I'm sure the boss will appreciate any support from former and future business pals."

Jesus, this lady doesn't have a clue, Ron thought. *If Paretti hears my line of bull that someone with connections to mob-connected Little Italy was here, he'll react with either interest or panic. The reaction will clue me in about what's going on in our crappy little town.*

Ron exited Starlet's Alley and kept a close watch on his former place of employment from a more hidden place across the street. He snacked on a Snickers bar and occasionally read excerpts from his Hammett novel, scanning the faces of those exiting and entering the parking lot for a few hours. His stakeout was even less glamorous than those Hammett had described.

Late into his surveillance, he noticed a silver Lincoln enter the lot. It was driven by a muscular, mustachioed man who could either be an insurance sales rep, a mobster, or both. The insurance or mob-employed goon got out and led a bandaged, beat-up Sal Paretti into the seedy strip joint.

Though the time was approaching quarter to eight in the evening, Ron watched the pair walk easily past the guards. He took a mental note of the driver and Paretti's condition before he sneaked into the parking lot.

Ron noticed that a number of tough guys exited the club after he grabbed a waiting taxicab. The bandaged Paretti soon followed and was mouthing about a "bitch waitress" and "Little Italy." He looked agitated to say the least. The mustachioed driver and a man with a mullet got into a black Lincoln shortly thereafter.

Ron had a date with a recently-hired Hooters

waitress and her kid. He didn't want to chance being late. He expected to run into the black Lincoln and its passengers shortly. He figured he would take care of problems as they came.

- - - - -

Carey tapped her fingers against the steering wheel at 8:13 as she waited for Ron to get to the Hooters parking lot. She stopped tapping when she saw a black Lincoln pull up. She watched tensely from the other side of the parking lot. She relaxed a bit when she saw her new roommate emerge a few minutes later from a taxi just down the road.

Thankfully, it looks like Ron sees the bastards too, Carey thought, waiting in her Corolla. *Wait, what in the hell is he doing*?

She smiled as she watched Ron creep up behind the Lincoln and plug the tailpipe with a large stick and leaves he had found in a nearby bush. He also stuck a knife into the Lincoln's back passenger's side tire and left it there as the driver and his passenger looked toward the Hooters for exiting waitstaff.

Carey giggled as he crept toward her car with a finger to his lips. He opened the door and entered quickly, telling her jokingly to be quiet. As the Corolla drove past the Lincoln and out of the parking lot, the Lincoln nearly stalled and pulled to the side of the road. Carey drove at a brisk fifty miles per hour to see her son. She gave Ron her Motorola Razr to call Lizzy to confirm the visit.

Carey's car returned to the posted speed when they came to the residential area of town.

Soon this unlikely gentleman will meet my boy and my best friend, she thought. *I can stop worrying for a little while, can't I*?

- - - - -

As the Corolla came within blocks of Lizzy's house, Ron told Carey to keep driving. He spotted a familiar, black Lincoln tailing them. Fortunately for them, their pursuers weren't subtle enough to go unnoticed.

"Don't even pull down the same street as Lizzy's house until we find out more about these jokers," he said. He got out one of his stolen Glock 9 mm semiautomatic handguns from a Walmart bag, handed it to her, and asked: "You know how to use this thing?"

"I may not have been in the Army," she said, "but I'm a single mom who's been cheated and threatened by losers who think they're tough. I lost my own piece when some greasy assholes burned my last rental down."

"I hope I'm not on your list of assholes," he said. "If you think of a good place to find out more about our tail, I'd appreciate it."

"You have some pleasant qualities. Chicks dig vulnerability with strength. Plus you cook a good breakfast. By the way, we're pretty near a stoplight by the Metra tracks if you want to take a closer look at these bozos. My Corolla can be rather prone to random breakdowns. We'll know more about our tail in the Lincoln if we get closer."

"We probably won't be able to outrun them. Let's give it a try," Ron said before Carey made the car sputter to a stop.

They both briefly held their breath as the black Lincoln came to a stop behind them. Ron wasn't sure yet if their move was dumb or not. By arming Carey, he wasn't taking more chances than he needed to. The familiar-looking, mullet-cut passenger from the Lincoln slowly ambled to the driver's side of the Corolla.

"I'll act clueless and ask if he has a jump," Carey said as the bulk of muscle and fat came toward them.

Ron's mouth opened slightly when she slid off the safety of the handgun, cocked it, and placed it in the crevice between her right leg and the stick shift. As she twirled her dark red hair with her left index finger, he admired her black yoga pants, form-fitting blue tank top. He realized he was getting distracted from the task at hand.

Once the mullet-cut goon was outside her door, he tapped his Smith & Wesson semiautomatic to the glass and motioned for her to bring the window down.

This is unfortunate, he thought, refocusing.

Carey started crying as if on command. Her left hand began to roll down the window as Ron adopted an annoyed look. He averted his eyes from those of the goon and shook his head. Her right hand, meanwhile, gripped the Glock and raised it in a split second before she shot the man point-blank in the chest.

The goon with the ugly haircut looked like he was about to take his own shot. He wasn't fast enough.

"Appear scared and helpless and that's what they'll expect," she said before putting the Corolla in reverse and vigorously bumping it into the front bumper of the black Lincoln behind them.

The Lincoln's driver blasted a few rounds that shattered the Corolla's rear window before his airbag went off. While he struggled with the bag, Ron exited the Corolla and fired two rounds into him to make him limp and silent. He recognized the mustache on the slack face.

Carey got out of the Corolla and started kicking the dead partner on the ground before Ron stopped her and searched for the wallets of their would-be assassins. He relieved them of $300, a Nokia cell phone, and an extra clip of 9 mm ammunition per body. He turned off the Nokia's GPS capability and powered down the phone before putting it in his pocket.

After taking the supplies, Ron gave Carey a tight hug and took her to the passenger's seat of the Corolla. He cleaned any possible fingerprints on the bodies and Lincoln before he returned to their car. He fought his own emotions and drove at a casual pace away from the scene.

Carey called Lizzy on her Motorola Razr, still shaking with rage, fear, or both.

"Lizzy, I'm sorry, but I'm not going to be able to come by even though we're probably less than a mile from where you live," she said. "There were violent men tailing us that we had to lose. My new friend and I are helping each other out of this mess. We don't want to put John, you, or your family in danger. We're fine now and working through this."

Ron heard a feminine voice coming through the receiver, excited but also relieved.

"Could you put John on the phone?" Carey asked. A few tears ran down her face as she listened to what Ron could only assume was John babbling the way a toddler does.

"I love you, baby," she said into her phone. "Sleep well and be good for Aunt Lizzy. I'll see you as soon as I can. Mommy has to take care of business first."

Carey thanked her friend and wished her a good night. Tears and mascara ran down her face before she took out a tissue and cleaned her cheeks and eyes. Ron thought she looked more vulnerable than ever before.

Ron headed slightly north to State Highway 34 and took it eastward. He looked out for any suspicious vehicles. For a Friday night, there weren't many cars, and all looked less sketchy than a Corolla with a crumpled bumper and a broken rear window. When he decided they were safe, they headed toward Carey's apartment.

He parked in a far part of the Walmart parking lot to avoid bringing any attention to the apartment. He would put a clear plastic sheeting over the smashed window when Walmart opened in the morning. He insisted that he would drive her from the Walmart and pick her up near her work to take the defensive against any more thugs.

Ron watched Carey's face before she nodded her head in agreement.

They took the Nokia, additional money and ammunition that they had taken from the goons and moseyed back to her place. He lay down next to her on the her twin mattress after they had changed into comfortable clothes and gotten ready for sleep. With her increasingly relaxed breaths, he was eventually satisfied that they were safe for now. He turned toward the wall and tried to sleep.

12

Complications

Carey Sullivan woke up suddenly and read 3:14 on her Motorola Razr after finding it next to her mattress. On her other side, she saw Ron sleeping, faced toward the wall. He was breathing deeply with his back to her, a trail of sweat on the nape of his neck. She didn't know what the exact situation was with him and her, but she liked him. He said he'd protect her and her son. He wanted her to meet his remaining family member. She'd never felt safer despite all the threats on her life.

Not having an answer can be exhilarating, she thought, *in a good way.*

She kissed him on the ear and waited for a response. When he turned around, she moved his right hand to her breasts. He kissed her on the cheek. A smile played across his lips as his eyes opened to focus hers. Soft moonlight filtered through the blinds.

"I want something more," she said in a voice that was lower and softer than usual.

"You're beautiful, Carey," he said. "I like you too, but I've got a lot of baggage–"

He stopped talking pretty quickly when her hand went into his boxer briefs. The only thing she mouthed in response to his apprehension was if it would be okay if they made love.

He nodded consent before responding to her touch.

Carey put her tongue between his lips as she explored under his muscular abdomen. He responded by putting his hand in her panties. They trembled and smiled in unison as they explored each other.

The air around them grew warm while they kissed as if they hadn't done so in years. He removed her oversize T-Shirt and underwear. She removed his boxer briefs and put a condom on him. After she climbed atop him and grabbed his waist with her toned thighs, he traced the palm of his right hand from her cheek to her shoulder.

Within forty-five minutes, they were both breathless after having climaxed. Ron nestled against Carey's healthy, firm hips and back shortly thereafter. They both had several hours of much-needed sleep before she awoke to the smell of French toast and smoked, spiced sausage in her kitchenette.

Ron was in his cargos and a black t-shirt, making breakfast while barefoot.

"For the love of Pete," she said. "I can make you breakfast for a change. You have to have more flaws besides an ease with killing people."

"I've been told I have trouble expressing myself," he said. "At least with words. And who the hell is Pete?"

She gave a light chuckle and rolled her eyes.

"Well, you had no trouble expressing yourself before the sun came up this morning," she said. "So verbal communication isn't your thing, huh?"

"Nope," he said before giving a lop-sided, toothy smile.

He sneaked a glance at her delectable body before she put on the over-sized t-shirt and joined him at the card table to eat. They ate without much chit chat. Carey played footsie under the table and Ron passed her coffee or syrup in response. After the meal, she insisted that he shower as she cleaned up and soaked the pans.

After putting the pans in the sink, she welcomed him outside the shower in nothing but her birthday suit. She went to kiss him slowly on the lips; her dark red hair framed her face as several stray waves ran teasingly down her graceful neck. He kissed her as his hand rubbed the small of her back where it met the curve of her behind. She returned the sentiment with a playful, if less than gentle spank.

Ron let her join him for the shower and more as they both wished they could have a more leisurely Saturday. Unfortunately, time wasn't on their side and they had to rush to don clothes before he could drive her to work. He dropped her off at 11:26, getting her door for her. She couldn't shake the kind but slightly worried look in his eyes as they said goodbye and went their separate ways.

Life just got more complicated, she thought after blowing a kiss.

- - - - -

Ron thought it was a pleasant morning. In the hour before Carey awoke, he went shopping for breakfast foods, a plastic sheet, duct tape, and other supplies. He wanted to fix up the car somewhat and get everything ready for when the red-haired beauty who had stirred him awoke from her slumber.

I was hesitant to talk with her a mere week ago. It shows how good a judge of character I am, he thought. *I didn't know how competent she was with a weapon...and in bed.*

As he drove her to her gig at the "Delightfully Tacky" restaurant, he gave her the phone numbers of both the Nokia taken off the dead passenger the previous night and that of a prepaid Samsung flip-phone that he had picked up on his morning shopping trip. He told her to call him if she ran into trouble before they met later that evening. She seemed to enjoy it when Ron held the door for her as she exited the increasingly disheveled Corolla.

What can I say, he thought. *I learned class from my aunt. Her other lesson was not to take any shit from anybody. That's another thing I won't forget.*

Before he returned to Carey's studio apartment, Ron stashed the Corolla in between a Hummer and another big car in the Walmart parking lot, blocked off from view by any major roads. This was the only time back stateside that he found a Hummer to be useful. He found them obnoxious when he returned from Iraq and saw "Support Our Troops" bumper stickers that had been made in China.

I'm not a damned liberal, he thought as he walked to the apartment, *but I had to fasten scrap metal on Humvees to fend against IEDs on roads back in the desert. A self-important Defense Department desk jockey told us to suck it up while wannabe hard-asses bought better equipped vehicles to drive in the burbs.*

Ron stopped his digression into frustration. After a few large breaths and muttering some words he usually reserved for degenerates and others like him, he decided to focus on the positive. He thought about the more pleasant early morning for the rest of the short walk to the apartment.

At Carey's, his mind focused on duty when he looked for familiar phone numbers in the memory of the dead thug's Nokia. There, he conveniently found S. Paretti and The Sicilian Boss. He copied the numbers on two pieces of scrap paper. He put one in his pocket with his wallet and he tucked the other under Carey's pillow should something happen to him.

She's a smart gal, he thought. *She'll figure something out between earning money and trying to stay alive.*

Ron then looked at the Nokia's media gallery to see if there was anything damning on any of the contacts. Only a snapshot of a teenage girl who was clearly coked up resonated with him. She looked like the former mayor's daughter, Kendra, whom he most recently saw in the *Sun-Times*. He didn't find it too surprising that she kept company with thugs and hitmen. What he did find somewhat interesting were pictures of someone with a similar-looking body straddling Sal Paretti. Only this time, the face was disguised in a mask.

The other thing that struck him was when he read the news and that there was no mention in the *Sun-Times*, nor the *Naperville Sun*, of two dead henchmen, killed relatively close to Lizzy's house. A trashed Lincoln was also unmentioned.

No doubt, people are getting paid off, he thought.

Ron powered down the Nokia before tucking it in with the note under Carey's pillow. He then drove the trashed Corolla to Naperville, hiding it outside the city's 95th Street Branch of the public library. At a public computer, he did a reverse phone lookup online to see if the number from the Nokia could identify The Sicilian Boss. He do a ProQuest search on Kendra De Silva, as well.

There's bound to be more dead bodies that go unnoticed, Ron thought to himself as he logged into the library's databases. *I have no*

- - - - -

Sal Paretti limped from a back room at Starlet's Alley as one of his longtime dancers took to the stage and peeled off a doctor's lab coat that barely hid her D-cup breasts. Two men, one in cowboy boots, a Bears sweatshirt and track pants, the other in Reebok high tops, acid-washed jeans, and a Bugle Boy t-shirt whooped and hollered. They were the classiest people in the club besides a bored bartender, four clueless bouncers, and some talent backstage. It was still early enough for the club to be slow.

Paretti's stomach shuddered like a fishbowl during an earthquake when he saw Nicholas Ferranti walk in with his Associate. He figured the latter was the masked person who stabbed and beat him the other night. He motioned for two bouncers to remain attentive as he joined his unwanted guests in a booth. He promptly ordered a fifth of Glenlivet for them and two aspirin with a fifth of Cuervo Silver for himself.

Ferranti had the temerity to ask how he was doing as the Associate simply blew him a kiss before carving into the table with a switchblade. The carvings were deep, slow, and undoubtedly deliberate.

"Just tell me what you want me to do," Paretti said, swishing down a dose of aspirin with a shot of tequila. "I need a bit of scratch. But I respectfully bow the hell out of any further dealings with anyone who nearly kills me before I do their bidding."

"But Mr. Paretti, we don't want you to go," Ferranti said after he took out a handkerchief and gave it to his host to wipe up a nosebleed.

"We could pay a steady hand half a grand per week to help us in this rough economy. But seeing as you don't have much of a choice, you'll settle for $400. Do we have a deal?"

"I thought you just wanted me to take the one hundred grand and scram." Paretti said after putting the slightly bloody handkerchief in his shirt pocket.

"Did I give that impression?" Ferranti asked. "I get frustrated and forget myself sometimes. We Sicilians are known for being hot under the collar. My friends in Chicago should take advantage, I mean respectfully defer, to local talent. You made a good point while playing hardball during our business meeting the other day."

Paretti drank another shot before he signed a transfer of ownership. He took another shot before signing a contract for his weekly allowance. He had one of the bouncers read all the documents to him. The Associate took a shot of Glenlivet and smirked as Ferranti calmly sipped his third dram neat.

"Remember, Sal," he said, "we know where to find you if you try and run out on our handsome deal."

Paretti toasted them with the bottle, doing without the shot glass. Ferranti and the Associate took the Glenlivet along with their leave as their new business partner drank tequila until only a third of the bottle was left. One of the bouncers took him back to his trailer as consciousness left. He listened to his boss' retching in a small sink before fetching bottled water from the club.

After awhile, the bouncer laid Paretti on his side in a bed. He and another bouncer helped themselves to the rest of the bottle of Cuervo before they wound down their official shift at two in the morning. It was then that they usually started to package cocaine for sale to local users and Chicagoland dealers.

Unfortunately for those plans, someone had snitched to the DuPage County Sheriff's Office from a Naperville pay phone earlier in the evening. No one bought cocaine with the sight of two cruisers in the parking lot.

- - - - -

Carey met Ron when he arrived in her Corolla outside Hooters after eight o'clock that evening, without incident. Her rusty, but trusty Toyota stuck out with its plastic rear window and crumpled bumper. She appreciated seeing Ron's confident eyes and a grin. He swung open the passenger's side door for her.

"I've got some theories about who is messing with our lives," he reported after greeting her. "You've run into Kendra De Silva?"

After Carey got in and he started driving, she told him again about their encounter. She had made the debutante drop her bottle of Jack before some goombahs escorted her rather willingly into a Mustang. Ron filled her in on the pictures that he saw, and how some further digging illuminated Kendra's problematic history with the law.

"I don't like to paint a teenager in a corner," he said. "It's our right to screw up at that age. Still, Kendra looks like she might be working with the assholes who took her pictures on the Nokia. The photographer and his buddy were likely connected to Chicago organized crime, based on their appearance and my research into Paretti's business dealings."

Carey listened as he explained that the

Nokia's phone number for the Sicilian Boss was mobile from Chicago. Ron called the number from a pay phone next to the library, but he only received by a polite, feminine voicemail greeting to "please leave a message at the tone."

Carey informed him that Woolrich city government had recently cut off all public access to cell phones of local staff and officials. This was officially due to security concerns. Investigative reporters, however, were interested in whether the mob syndicate was demanding power from local politicians.

The tight cheekbones and wide eyes on Ron's more than mildly astonished face made Carey giggle.

"What? I get the news from WGN radio and looking at the *Sun-Times* when my co-workers are done with it," she said. "I wouldn't be surprised if our interim mayor might have some deal with the Chicago mob, even though the official story is that he's clean."

She smiled when Ron nodded and quipped that the mob and most politicians only differed in who could legitimately play with local tax dollars.

On the ride to her apartment, she asked him to stop at a gas station, where she picked up a fifth of Jack Daniels. They hid the Corolla in the Walmart lot by a trashed Buick and walked back to her apartment, happy to have a chance to unwind.

"Should we go to someone with our information?" Carey asked back in her kitchenette as she poured them both a few fingers of whiskey in Hooters coffee mugs.

"We should probably wait until we figure out more," he said. "For now, I'm collecting information that may be useful if we, by chance, can talk to clean cops who want to find out what's going on. I phoned in an anonymous tip today to the DuPage County Sheriff at a pay phone outside the library to rattle Paretti. That's as close as I'll go to the fuzz for now."

They exchanged smiles as Carey's cheeks started to blush. She agreed with him and changed the subject. She focused on the logistics of possibly seeing her son in the next couple of days. She wanted to bring John to meet Aunt Peggy.

She poured them another two fingers of Jack before they toasted and laughed like any lighthearted couple. Only after an hour did they grow more serious. They worried over clearing their names, making the guilty accountable, and being with their loved ones again in peace. After she slipped into a clean, oversize T-shirt, Ron stripped to a clean set of boxer briefs and joined her on her mattress. He wrapped his left arm around her abdomen.

Carey nestled into his firm frame, listening to both their breathing before falling asleep for eight hours. She was more than happy to be woken with fresh coffee and a bowl of generic Wheaties before getting ready for her Sunday shift later that morning. Ron even thought to pick up the "freshest blueberries Walmart has to offer."

"Faced with bad guys, crooked cops, lecherous losers, and coked up spoiled brats, it's the sweet little things that make life bearable," she said, kissing him on the lips. He later dropped her off in the trashed Toyota. They were both grinning when they parted ways.

Goodness, Carey thought as she walked toward the Hooters, *was that optimism in his eyes?*

13

Fugitive

Mayor De Silva's widow, Anne, learned just after dawn that her defense lawyer had died of a "cardiac event" the night before. The bail bondsman hired by DuPage County informed her of the news before he escorted her to breakfast at the Holiday Inn Express just outside western Woolrich. She had been there since withdrawing most of her and her late husband's joint savings to post bail.

Anne hadn't heard from her children since police took them away. She was sure that Tom and Bryan were safe enough with relatives. Kendra had never shown any vulnerability, nor obedience, since turning fifteen. Her mom suspected that she had a drug habit with something harder than booze or cannabis.

A mother still worries, she thought to herself, taking out her pack of Virginia Slims only to be escorted outside by bondsman, Dan Jurecki. She was angry that she had to step outside to smoke. She was at least happy her husband was dead so she could maybe get Kendra into treatment without upsetting any voters.

I also can't get used to the fact that I can't smoke a legal drug indoors except in my home, she thought. *Goddamn it, why couldn't have my husband have been a state representative? He was a friend of the Speaker. Mike Madigan would've worked with Governor Blagojevich for my full pardon by now.*

"Blagojevich will likely be facing his own trial in due time," Anne muttered under her breath after she took a drag and exhaled sweet carcinogens into the air. "If anything, he deserves to go to jail instead of me. Corruption is bipartisan at least–"

"Ma'am, I'd ask you to not mention anything about the man giving subsidies for my salary," Jurecki said.

Pansy, Anne thought.

To be fair to Jurecki, he did offer Anne a light and ask if she needed anything else before he had to change shifts with another bondsman. She had been following him as much as he had been her. She knew his routine, she knew what weapons he had on him, and she knew where his car was. All she needed was a calm attitude, and the cigarette helped.

"Thanks for the light," she said, before she stabbed her cigarette into his neck and kneed him in the testicles. Before he could begin to process what was happening, Anne brought the full force of her fist into his temple, knocking him unconscious. She relieved him of his Sig Sauer semiautomatic, his keys, and the $50 in his wallet before swiftly sprinting to his maroon 2003 Ford Taurus.

"Well, I've never done anything like this before," Anne said to herself, before speeding out of the parking lot. "Sorry Jurecki, but this is exhilarating. I haven't felt this free since fleeing the house after someone knocked off my husband."

Anne De Silva headed east toward Woolrich at twice the pace of anyone out for a lazy Sunday drive. Once back in her city, she lowered her speed, lay low, relied on friends, and tried to look into the goings-on of her daughter.

Tom and Bryan will be fine, she thought. *Boys get away with so much more.*

- - - - -

Sal Paretti did not feel free. He felt like his head and his testicles were both in a vice at the same time. He guessed that he should have appreciated the efforts of one of his bouncers to help him through his drunk to feel so miserable. But actually, he didn't. He shot the man in the face after seeing him outside his dilapidated trailer eight hours earlier, just before noon.

I'm not gonna bother working today, Paretti thought while the evening rush started. *Where are my tits and ass when I need them, Goddammit? When I'm hungover, boobies in my face make me feel better.*

Paretti nearly stained his pants when he heard the honk of the Sicilian's Lincoln after it stopped just outside of his trailer. He quickly tried to get out of his stupor before answering the door. He didn't realize how poorly he smelled.

Although the Sicilian's only back-up was his driver, he proceeded to pummel first on Paretti's door and then on the latter's large gut.

"What gives, boss?" Paretti said with a slack-jawed, furrow-browed expression after he had regained his breath. "I sold the place to you. I agreed to be the middle-man. What the hell else do you want?"

The Sicilian put his hand almost all the way around Paretti's neck and gripped his carotid artery with an index finger. He squeezed firmly from time to time.

"My Associate informed me about two DuPage County Sheriff cruisers that were parked outside my strip club from two to four this morning," he said. "You should have been the one to tell me about it. I would've been able to call off or distract the dogs. The staff you are supposed to manage could have moved some product."

Paretti just gasped for air when the Sicilian released his fingers.

"Who in God's name do you think you are, Sal?" he asked. "I not only own your soul, your business, and any relevance you think you had, I own the city council, the county board, and several state legislators. You can drink yourself near death every night. Just respect the fact that I ultimately control who lives or dies here."

"Yes, sir," Paretti said with a subdued, morbid look of a dog who had just been neutered.

"Now tell me, jerk off," the Sicilian said, "did Carey Sullivan give you a forwarding address for her paychecks? The guy who doles out your paychecks would like to know if we can cut some overhead."

"She gave me the address of a Red Lobster in Naperville after her apartment burned down," Paretti said. "I know, like you probably do, that she's working at the Hooters. If I knew something different, would I hold back information?"

"That's a good question," he said before he led Paretti to the trailer's shower and sent four well-armed men in a black Cadillac over to the local Hooters.

When one of Woolrich's police officers later arrived at Starlet's Alley, he was paid to say that he found Paretti with a broken neck in the shower of his trailer, cool water still running over his stout, naked body. The officer didn't find any evidence of foul play. A slick sheen of soap under the deceased hinted that Paretti had merely slipped and fell. The bouncers all gave statements that their late boss was an alcoholic.

The Sicilian sipped on Glenlivet from his booth and watched the bouncers talk to the cop. His biggest regret was that after-hours coke deals would be off the table for the night due to any possible police scrutiny from those not bribed. He decided to send an additional, silver Cadillac with two goons to report on the other four's progress with the stripper problem. The extra two were to tie up loose ends if need be.

I like to play things safe, he thought. *Maybe the good Mayor Peck will say something at Paretti's funeral. I'll be there to offer my condolences, from one caring local business owner to another.*

- - - - -

Ron noticed the black Cadillac enter the Hooters parking lot about five minutes before Carey's shift was through. The crinkled Corolla was parked across from the parking lot. He had his Samsung, his Glock, and two of four steak knives he had bought at Walmart that morning in case he needed something cheap and sharp. He had had a busy day, keeping up with the news and subtly stalking the new mayor, Rob Peck. He wanted to relax with some fingers of a freshly bought fifth of Jim Beam that rested in a paper bag on the passenger's seat.

The Cadillac made him realize that his day was going to get busier.

Ron gave Carey a call on her Motorola Razr. She picked up without saying anything.

Good response, he thought.

He told her about the possible heat gathered outside and told her to stay inside the Hooters, where she would be safer. He crept up behind the Cadillac and sabotaged it with stabs to the back tires, leaving the knives in to stem immediate airflow. He got back to the beat-up Corolla and started the engine to make a quicker escape. He watched two of the men get out of the Cadillac's back seat. Both had big dark-colored coats that could hide a decent amount of firepower.

Jeez, these guys are really overdoing it going after a waitress at Hooters, he thought. *With a number of these idiots now dead, they likely feel the need to overcompensate. Good thing I still have an advantage with all my tires intact.*

Ron shot just above the head of one of the men approaching the Hooters and fired close enough to the other one for him to shout a four-letter word. They both ran back to the Cadillac, shooting in Ron's direction. A pair of headlights sputtered toward the Corolla. Ron was already at the wheel and starting down the road in front of his very angry pursuers.

Ron realized that he had to slow down so that the Cadillac could follow him. He led them to Highway 34, exchanging fire from time to time. About a mile before the on-ramp, he realized that the Jim Beam would more immediately help him as an improvised Molotov cocktail. Unhappy with logic, he unscrewed the top, stuffed a wad of the paper bag in the neck of the bottle, and lit the paper with the cigarette lighter once in popped out.

Out of the driver's side window, Ron tossed his homemade explosive toward the tailing vehicle as he got onto highway. With help from a few blasts from his Glock, his pursuers crashed into a divider before the Cadillac burst into flames. Ron returned to Hooters at the maximum velocity his trashed, yet still functioning, Japanese car carried him.

When he got back toward Carey at quarter to nine, he called her and instructed her to meet him a few hundred feet down the road from the Hooters. He finally took a full breath after he saw her walking toward him. He started to relax somewhat when he saw that she hadn't suffered any physical harm.

She got in the car, and Ron began an elusive route back to her apartment. He studied his surroundings at every intersection and every long stretch of road for anything suspicious. He swore when he saw a silver Cadillac following.

The Cadillac was getting aggressive, coming within two car lengths of the rapidly accelerating Corolla. When Ron saw a handgun emerge from the driver side, he gave his Glock to Carey. She removed her seat belt and carefully climbed in the back seat to remove the temporary covering of the rear window. The discarded plastic covering flew back to make the Cadillac swerve before two stray shots hit the Corolla's bumper. When their pursuer stabilized, Carey shot rounds into the driver's side front wheel and headlights,

Both she and Ron breathed a sigh of relief when the Cadillac made an abrupt turn into a ditch. When they got back to the Walmart, Ron parked along the edge of the lot. They took a walk through a small grassy area to clear their heads.

"So...how was your day," she said after a while.

Ron gently grabbed her waist with his left hand, turned her toward him, and kissed her on the lips. She responded in kind.

"This is the highlight of my day," he said. "It wasn't that great before, having to shadow a politician, research the news, and blow up a car full of hostiles. You know, the usual. I need a drink. You?"

"You're much nicer than the lecherous locals I serve all day," she said, putting her right hand on his chest. "Same old perverts, meatheads, and shy businessmen trying to look powerful, Let's head home for a special treat."

Back at the studio apartment, she heated Dinty Moore beef stew on her stove top and served it in to-go bowls she had nabbed from work. She also got each of them two heavy drams of the remaining Jack Daniels and turned on a small radio just as Frank Sinatra started to croon "The Way You Look Tonight." She danced with the beat of the song while bringing over the drinks.

After they were done dining, she undressed and put on her oversize T-shirt in front of him. She motioned him to go to the twin mattress before she washed up the kitchenette. When she joined him, she massaged his shoulders before she he nestled her backside against him. The sound of her breathing lulled him to sleep as his hands rested on the curve of her behind.

14

Bad News, Good Friends

Nicky Ferranti's Naperville basement was cold in the first hour of Monday morning despite the tan leather couch and entertainment system meant to make it more cozy. Most of the iciness came from Ferranti, who would pay off or take out anyone who interrupted the Chicago Mob's business. Incompetent subordinates were as disposable as spent brass.

"I swear, boss," said the gap-toothed passenger of the silver Cadillac that Carey had shot at the previous evening. "I saw the Corolla that sped off with me on its tail. I don't know what else to tell you except that our mark drove like a maniac and that stripper had good aim. They know the lay of the land, and you know that we ain't locals."

"So you're saying that this is my fault?" Ferranti asked. "Well, then the hell with you."

"Boss, I didn't mean to say that at all," he said. "We just weren't able to follow them any further after she shot out our tire. My driver died when we hit a ditch. What could I have done differently?"

"So your excuse is that you are incompetent. Well, that's just brilliant, isn't it? I'm afraid I'm gonna have to let you go."

Ferranti cut off further discussion when he gave the gap-toothed thug a third eye with a bullet from his Ruger. He relished the fear his Sicilian mannerisms and high-powered handguns commanded. He turned to three recently transplanted thugs from Chicago who had been watching the scene. The sight of their tight jaws and unblinking eyes pleased him.

"I hope you assholes can be of better service to me than that failed tail," he said. "The Corolla in question is registered to Carey Sullivan's former apartment. Public records put a Verizon cell phone number as the home phone number. One of the local cops on my dole requested the records from Verizon. He cited national security to help us out.

"That's as far as the copper will go," he continued. "You jokers have to check the phone records to see if there's an address that she has called or threaten those Verizon geeks into triangulating a general location. That may help us flush out Sullivan and McCallister. Those two have already killed a half dozen or so gunmen; don't give me more cause to add to that body count."

The three goons nervously agreed to help. They would have to distinguish a pattern of calls, which may or may not impress Ferranti. They had to try their best in order to not lose their lives or worse.

The Sicilian, Nicky Ferranti, planned to catch a few hours of shut-eye while his goons worked. The tan leather couch, a low-ball glass of Glenlivet, and the darkness of the basement made the onset of sleep come quicker.

- - - - -

Carey called her friend, Lizzy at around 9 a.m., having recovered somewhat from the chase and shootout the night before. Lizzy agreed to meet her, with John, at a public park near her house. The Corolla stopped just before noon about a block from the park.

As Carey met her friend, Ron kept watch in the distance. He minded the car with a Glock in his sweatshirt pocket. The chamber was empty and the safety was engaged. Carey's gun was similarly disposed and locked in the glove compartment.

At the park, the two friends exchanged a warm hug after Lizzy released the hand of her son, Brian. Shortly after Carey patted Brian on the head, she embraced her son and lifted him into her arms. She gleefully swung John around and kissed him softly on his healthy, chubby cheeks. John giggled with glee.

"Thank you so much, Lizzy," Carey said. "I don't know where I'd be without your help. I've brought a bottle of Cabernet Sauvignon for you and your hubby to share tonight while I watch John. Will it be okay if he stays with you for a few more days after tonight until I get more issues settled?"

"Hon, your boy keeps my Brian occupied. He can stay as long as he needs to," Lizzy said before she glanced toward the Corolla. "Say, is that the killer stud sitting in your car? Looks like the Toyota has had some action, and with your calmness in spite of all this, I'd guess that you've had some action as well."

Carey gave an ironic grimace toward her friend before responding.

"He cooks, cleans, and kills bad guys. He's wanted for a few felonies, committed in self-defense, but he's all mine for now. And he's taking my son and I to meet his aunt. That other part is no one else's business."

"The little beard he's got going on is kinda cute, in that beatnik boyfriend sort of way. Other than an ability to kill people, he has what every woman wants in a domesticated man. My Mike has a great job as one of Mayor Peck's communications director and he's a good father, so I can't complain either."

"Well, I don't have a life that anyone should covet. But I have a wonderful son and always have enough gumption to get out of the rough spots. You take Brian and have a good night with Mike, now. I love you and thank you so much for all of your help."

Carey hugged her friend again. Lizzy walked toward her house with Brian while Carey and John joined Ron in the car. He revealed a brown teddy bear and handed it to John.

"Used some stolen mob money to pick this up for you, little guy," Ron said.

John didn't get the joke, of course, but gave a broad smile while taking the bear.

Carey poked Ron in the ribs while she rolled her eyes. Her two guys, one bigger and the other smaller, gave each other high fives before they all drove like one happy family to Naperville. Aunt Peggy was expecting company.

- - - - -

Ferranti debated with himself whether or not he should put the squeeze on the wife of someone who worked at City Hall since Mayor Peck was such a useful collaborator. He reassured himself that he was the one who ran the show. He was taking the reins of Woolrich business for the mob, so he figured he knew what was best.

He broke into Lizzy Simmons' place while no one was home, entering through a window in the backyard. Her husband was out dealing with the press for Mayor Rob Peck, and she had just left to take her son and some other brat for a walk.

It wasn't like the mob wanted to draw more press to Woolrich's political elite, but Ferranti's three goons selected this place from their quick, yet effective, Verizon phone records research. He gulped a few shots of Southern Comfort that he found in the cupboard to try to relax while waiting for Lizzy.

I sure as shit didn't want an average asshole hitman to help me with this, Ferranti thought. *My Associate is too nuts to not just set the whole place on fire. Sometimes the leader's gotta do the dirty work.*

When he heard the keys working to unlock the front door, he got behind the cupboard attached to the kitchen entrance. When the door opened, he sneaked up behind Lizzy and smacked her on the back of the head with the butt of his Ruger.

"What the hell?!" she asked, letting go of her small boy's hand. "Run, Brian! Run! Go tell the neighbors!"

Brian, though only four years old, stopped when he saw the stranger in his house knock his mother unconscious and then point a handgun at him.

"Say, you're pretty smart for a kid," Ferranti said. "You know to stop and listen up when you got a gun pointed at you or your stupid mother."

Ferranti shook the boy's mother for emphasis as the kid raised his hands and started crying. Their captor promptly zip-tied Lizzy's hands behind her back. In an attempt to keep the boy placid, he put Beauty and the Beast in the DVD player. He made microwave popcorn and gave the boy milk, spiked with a little Southern Comfort. He helped himself to the wine that Lizzy had been carrying. Ferranti's kept his gun concentrated on the door of the Simmons' house as he sipped. He slowly got tipsy with junior and waited for Lizzy to wake up.

When Lizzy's eyes opened again, her captor wasn't pleased with her lack of information. Ferranti found it suspect, since Carey had contacted her phone number several times in the past days. His goons had confirmed the calls.

"I'm telling you she hasn't let on about specifics, nor have I asked her about any," she said. "The only thing I know is that she's getting help from that bouncer guy who escaped from the hospital last week, she has her son, and she's happy. What the hell else would I know?"

Ferranti was displeased and almost drunk, which led him to be violent. He grabbed Lizzy by the throat, squeezing as Brian grew increasingly agitated and started throwing Duplo blocks at his head. Brian stopped and peed his pants when he heard the piercing sound of a gun shot that resulted in Duplo shards flying across the room.

Ferranti knocked Lizzy unconsciousness with a dose of phenobarbital before he abducted her. He tied Brian's arms to the boy's torso and left him crying in front of the television. He left about a half hour before Lizzy's husband, Mike, came home. The only note he left was his cell phone number. It was taped to Brian's back.

When Mike Simmons got back from the mayor's office, he grew anxious when he heard his son crying inside. What he saw when he entered didn't help his mood. After Brian was untied, he went around the house to look for Lizzy. The only clue he found about what happened to his family was the phone number.

"If the mob has anything to do with this, not only will they have a vigilante bouncer out to kill them," Mike said, "but I will personally see to it that anyone who hurts my wife or son will end up six feet underground."

Mike first thought about calling 911, but didn't. He instead called on a friend at the Chicago office of the FBI. He didn't trust the Woolrich police with this. As communications director at City Hall, he had seen some damning things in Mayor Peck's office. The Feds had better resources to deal with kidnapping and any characters in organized crime.

His friend, FBI Agent Matt Russo, answered after the first ring.

- - - - -

Aunt Peggy was happy to see visitors, even if she hadn't met them before. A fit redhead entered her room. The visitor was holding the hand of a pleasantly chubby toddler with a tuft of matching red curls atop his head.

"Hello," she said. "The cranks who run this place said I was to get visitors, but I'm afraid we haven't yet met."

"Well, please excuse any intrusion, ma'am. I'm Carey Sullivan and this is my son, John," the gal said. "I'm a close friend of your nephew, Ron, and–"

"Hold on, sweetie," Aunt Peggy interrupted. "I gotta see you better now that you said you're a friend of my favorite nephew. Fetch the glasses on end table for me and fix them up on my head."

Carey did as told.

"I'm happy to learn that Ron finally found a nice gal, but he's outdone himself on finding one with such class," Aunt Peggy said. "But if you're really sweet on my Ronnie, you'll know what he always brings me and know where you can get the board for my favorite game. If you know what to do, you oughta call me Aunt Peggy."

She then called a nurse to get her friend, Ervin, and was pleased to see that Carey was well-informed. Carey brought out the pint of Jameson that Ron had bought and put a few fingers of the golden liquid in some Styrofoam cups.

"Ron tells me that you keep the cribbage board under your mattress," Carey said softly into her ear. "Would you like me to get it for you?"

Aunt Peggy nodded and smiled as a nurse wheeled Ervin into the room. She introduced him to Carey and John before Ervin nodded his head to each. He smiled before grabbing one of the drams of Jameson.

"Well, my nephew must have told you what to do," Aunt Peggy said. "I understand that Ron probably can't visit on account of pot-licker policemen and politicians trumping up charges against him. But like I said, I'm glad he sent you, sweetheart. You play cribbage? If not, Ervin here will teach you."

"I'm afraid I don't know how to play cribbage, Aunt Peggy," Carey said. "But I'd be honored if Ervin taught me."

Ervin didn't talk much, but he presented the rules as best he could over the Jameson, and he and Carey played a couple rounds with their cards face up. Aunt Peggy, meanwhile, recited limericks as John clapped along. A recently-hired, friendly nurse helped keep her from spilling any whiskey.

"Such a dear child, Carey," Aunt Peggy said. "It takes a good mother to raise such a charmer. You must put your son first."

"Ron says that is what you did for him," Carey said. "My son comes first, and your nephew seems to respect that. He said his Aunt Peggy raised him right."

Aunt Peggy smiled and gave a wink with her right eye before turning her attention back to John.

After Carey got the hang of cribbage, she and Aunt Peggy played a couple of rounds. Peggy skunked her the first time, but she beat her opponent by only five points the next round. Carey declined more whiskey but gamely poured more rounds for Aunt Peggy and Ervin.

Ervin was having a good time teaching John "Patty Cake" and showing a magic trick where he appeared to remove his thumb from his hand. After over a half hour, he blew kisses goodbye to the ladies and tousled John's hair before he called a nurse to wheel him back to his room.

"I've never had such a close game with a new player before," Aunt Peggy said after their second game. "That my boy would attract a gal who is not only a good-looking but smart makes my heart glad."

"It's truly been an honor, Aunt Peggy," Carey said. "Ron says only wonderful things about you."

"Well, dear, I hope he gets things cleared up with those dummies I read about in the papers. I'd really love to see him before I check out. But I give you all a kiss on the forehead for now. I'm so happy you stopped by."

Carey put the cribbage board back in its place. She pecked Aunt Peggy on the cheek after getting her settled. John was trying to recite the limericks that he had been taught when they got up to leave.

- - - - -

Ron picked them up in the early evening and

listened about their visit, getting a kiss on the forehead from Aunt Peggy through Carey. He was barely able to hold back the tears in his eyes while they headed back to her apartment

When they returned home, he excused himself and stepped downstairs and outside to vent and take some deep breaths. He returned ten minutes later to join Carey and John for SpaghettiOs. Around nine, Carey put John on her mattress and tucked him in before she and Ron headed back outside to take in the early spring air. Ron held a Hooters coffee cup with a healthy two fingers from a fresh fifth of Jack Daniels.

"Thanks again for seeing my dear Aunt Peggy," he said. "She means the world to me."

"Don't mention it," she said. "She's lovely. She and her friend, Ervin, were wonderful to John. If we get things figured out, we should all take trip to see both of them and spend some time together."

Ron sipped his whiskey and nodded his head as they took in the all-too-rare minutes of quiet. His face grew taut as he gazed across the parking lot to the grasslands and seemingly peaceful foliage beyond. He decided to focus on immediate tasks where he could make a difference.

"Per some current research, the current mayor is likely connected to the Chicago mob," he said. "So it's gonna take some doing to find justice. I'd wager Nicky Ferranti is calling hits on us when he's not working drug distribution or local real estate."

Ron filled her in on findings from a library visit while she and John were at Lavender Springs. Their former boss was dead without any official suspicions of foul play. To him, this only opened up more questions about Ferranti and the pull organized crime held on the town. A *Naperville Sun* editorial poked holes in Mayor Rob Pecks reputation as a reformer.

"Why the hell did my son and I settle here?" Carey asked.

"There's politics and corruption almost everywhere," Ron responded. "We're on the right side and we'll have to figure it out. We have an idea of who the bad guys are, so we'll react as events unfold. It might be better to have a firm mindset than a firm plan."

"Are you a soldier or a philosopher?" she asked after a few minutes.

"Both," he responded, trying to lighten the mood with a poke to her firm right bicep. "Chicks dig both even though neither make the big bucks. Why is that?"

She embraced him and met his lips with hers. He put his arm around her shoulder and they took in the placid atmosphere before returning inside. Carey joined her son on her twin mattress while Ron found a space on the floor next to them. He used the clothing he'd acquired as a pillow. With relative ease, they all found sleep.

15

Politicians, Criminals, Hitmen

Mayor Rob Peck had been sleeping soundly next to his wife in their Frank Lloyd Wright-style house when he heard his Blackberry buzz at 4:13 Tuesday morning. He groaned when he realized it was coming from the Metropolitan Correctional Center in Chicago. He promptly silenced the phone and ducked downstairs in the kitchen so he wouldn't have an audience.

When he arrived in the kitchen, Peck washed down two Bayer tablets with a gulp from a fifth of Tito's vodka. He tried to figure out who would be calling from the federal prison facility. He answered the phone when it buzzed again a few minutes later, simply mumbling his last name as a greeting. He recognized the voice from WGN news.

"Mr. Mayor, the Feds may have found me guilty, but I'm still waiting for sentencing. I'm calling you to let you know that one of the mob bosses may have gone after the wife of your Communications Director Mike Simmons. He probably won't hurt her if he knows what's good for him. But you might have to do exactly what I say if you want to stay on as mayor and keep your sterling reputation. And it is sterling, by the way."

Chicago mob boss, Joey "the Clown" Lombardo, had somehow gotten Mayor Peck's number. Lombardo was waiting to be sentenced for convictions stemming the FBI's Operation Family Secrets investigation. The phone call supported Peck's growing fears that the FBI was expanding inquiries into Woolrich.

"How do I know that this phone isn't tapped, and that you're not making some sort of deal with the Feds?" Peck asked. "I can't do anything to keep you out of the penitentiary. Don't involve me in anything criminal."

"I still say I'm innocent, but no one will believe me." Lombardo replied. "Well, I guess the only guarantee an allegedly powerful man behind bars can give is that you still have your life and the lives of your kid and your wife. You're also free to walk away, step down, if you can't handle the heat from criminals who just happen to be in my social circle. I hear that Vegas needs more bouncers and croupiers for gambling houses and strip clubs, if you're interested. It's honest work, if you don't mind the pay cut."

"What can I do for you, Mr. Lombardo?" Peck asked.

"It's not what you can do for me. It's what you can do for your family and my family. You remember the message from a cousin that you oughta look out for the interests of a Sicilian friend. Well, other cousins are thinking of who could run for mayor when you're done with Mayor De Silva's term. If you continue to help them, you could maybe run unopposed in the next election."

Lombardo explained further in code that Mayor Peck would have to display a veneer of control over the situation and the city while relinquishing some actual control. Peck was to announce that the whereabouts of his communications director's wife, Lizzy Simmons, was unknown, but that there was no suspected foul play. Peck should keep the Sicilian boss, Nicky Ferranti, and the mob's role under wraps, stay quiet, and assure the public that he had things under control.

"Ferranti is *de facto* the major player in the city as long as he keeps his business, more or less, copacetic with the lovely Woolrich community. If you still hold your own and keep any undue fuzz off of our boy Nicky, you and your family may still benefit from the best lifestyle in town. If you don't have the *coglionis*, changes in profession are commonplace with the tough job market."

Mayor Peck took a second gulp of Tito's before responding.

"I'll maintain my resolve to fight criminals," he said. "But your man, Ferranti, will not likely get any unwanted attention if he handles his business affairs discreetly. The Simmons family prefers to handle family issues privately."

"That sounds like it'll win over a lot of people who still believe in the system," Lombardo said. "I'll give you a choice bit of info that some associates are not giving Nicky; if he doesn't work harder to keep us out of the eye of the general public, a new underling the family sent might be able to take over Starlet's Alley as quickly as a shot from a sniper rifle.

"A hit on a prosperous politician like yourself, on the other hand, might be too conspicuous for criminals who may be colleagues, if not my closest ones."

Mayor Peck gulped down any nervousness, but decided against another shot of Tito's. He politely asked Lombardo if he needed anything else. He was met with a menacing chuckle before being told to go back to bed and cuddle with his comely wife. Peck went up the stairs and tried to settle next to Woolrich's first lady. With her soft breath on his neck, he lied awake in silence until the alarm at seven thirty a.m. told them to start their day.

- - - - -

Nicky Ferranti watched his Associate punch a blindfolded Lizzy Simmons in the belly the morning after she was kidnapped. The three were with several goons and other mob help at a hideout in nearby Lisle. Kendra De Silva had no qualms with doling out punches or worse. Ferranti thought that she would betray her own mother if her cocaine supply was threatened.

A drug addict will always forgo loyalty to feed a habit, he thought. *You can count on that more than a mother's love. Both are beautiful things, but one incentive is more reliable than the other in the Associate's case.*

He gave Kendra a line of cocaine before he put some underneath Lizzy's nose as the latter lay on the oak floor of the red-brick, one-story structure. He eventually told his new underling from Chicago, Gino Drucci, to put Lizzy in the cellar. She found no comfort on the cold concrete.

Ferranti figured she would probably be useful later. He ordered two goons to keep her alive, if not well.

"We are focused on more long-term gains," he said to Drucci and anyone else who was listening. "You take unnecessary risks if you openly knock off the loved ones of those access to power. Isn't that right, sweetheart?"

Kendra just snorted more cocaine off of Ferranti's firm forefinger. He smiled at the way the mob's situation got more complicated despite his self-confidence. He had gotten his go-ahead from Joey Lombardo earlier that morning to "make things happen while trying to keep an even keel."

He put a line of cocaine on the kitchen table of the hideout and snorted it off. The stimulation made him feel like he had a God-like position in local affairs. Reveling in his hubris, he decided to call two hoodlums outside of the local Hooters and order them to give Mike Simmons a good scare.

One of Ferranti's friends in the police department said the communications director was asking inconvenient questions. Simmons inquired particularly about disregarded 911 calls from Friday and Sunday evenings. He told the mob's cordially connected cop that several constituents personally contacted him about gun shots and explosions. Simmons was cautious enough to not name the concerned citizens.

"We gotta send Mike Simmons a message, but make it look to the press like an accident," he instructed the two hoodlums at the Hooters. "Drive by his house and take out his mailbox when he goes to check it. Don't hit him but get close enough to make him piss his pants. If anything goes wrong, don't bother staying in the state. My occasional bowling buddy, Governor Blagojevich, won't help you."

Ferranti hung up before sniffling abruptly and giving a hearty laugh. He reveled in the image of his two henchmen sweating bullets before they'd have to carry out their task. The cocaine made him cockier than he ought to have been.

16

A Chance to Hit Back

Carey called Lizzy's mobile phone later that Tuesday morning at 10:34, but she was only met with a voicemail greeting. When she dialed Lizzy's house phone, Mike picked up. His soft, staccato baritone voice hinted at worry.

"Mike, this is Carey Sullivan," she said, wondering why he wasn't at City Hall. "I was calling to check in with Lizzy. Is there something the matter?"

Mike told her about Lizzy's disappearance and meeting an inconsolable, tied-up Brian at home the previous evening. He told her that he hadn't slept in over twenty-four hours and asked if she might be able to shed some light on what happened. The only clue that he found was a phone number taped to his son's back.

"I'll be right over, Mike," she said. "Just don't do anything rash to put you or Brian at risk. I have a friend who may be able to help us. Give me the phone number from the note."

Carey wrote the number on a slip of paper before hanging up. She tapped Ron on the shoulder as he was completing his fiftieth push-up. He gave a grimace, squinted his eyes in slight annoyance, but was still receptive. He stretched his arms over his shoulders as he looked her in the eye.

"We have an emergency at the Simmons household," she said. "I'll keep John safe in the car if you could help look into what's happened to Lizzy. Her husband, Mike, was on the phone. She's missing and the only possibly solid piece of evidence is a phone number."

Carey's eyes widened with Ron's as he took in the information. He immediately looked for the Nokia phone that he had nabbed a few days ago. She joined his side as their minds clicked. She gave him a piece of scratch paper with the number.

Carey watched as Ron checked the Nokia's contacts and smirked in recognition. He went immediately for the Glock 9 mm semiautomatics, which were kept in a higher cupboard next to the whiskey out of John's reach. He handed her one of the gins.

"Is it what I think it is?" she asked.

"That's the number for the Sicilian Boss," he said. "We should get a move on to help your friend. Get John and let's head to the car."

Carey wasted no time retrieving her son before they all went to the Corolla. After buckling John in the back seat, putting her Glock in the glove compartment, and fastening her own seat belt, Ron drove off as swiftly as he could.

- - - - -

Ron pulled the damaged, rusty Corolla down the block on the other side of the street from Mike Simmons' doorstep. He noticed a Honda Accord with two stout guys cruising down the same street as he rang the doorbell. Carey huddled with John in the back seat, alarmed by the car. The Accord paid no overt attention to the Simmons household, but went past at about fifty miles per hour.

"I think you should tell your boy, Peck, to post more speed limit signs," Ron said after Mike Simmons and he exchanged hellos through the three inches separating the door from its frame. "Though I doubt tough-looking hard-asses obey traffic signs."

"What are you talking about?" Mike asked.

"Some tough guys sped by here a few seconds ago in a car that looks too economical for two grown men who don't have anywhere to be. Call it a hunch, but after your wife disappeared, you and Brian are likely in a tight spot with mobsters or other thugs run amok. I'm a friend of Carey Sullivan. No time to argue. Wave me off and walk to the end of the driveway and wait there after you check for mail. Leave Brian in the house where he's farthest away from the road. You can stay as bait when I take care of these assholes."

"Why should I trust you?"

"Carey is in the shitty-looking Corolla down the way. She and her kid will probably be the only people alive that I will care about in a matter of weeks. I'm not about to let them down by letting you, your wife, your son, or me die today. Is that good enough reason for you?"

"What choice do I have?"

"Not much of one. So, just help all of us out by being bait and letting me work my magic. If you hear a gunshot, run like hell away from the road and you'll probably live too."

Mike nodded before Ron ran across the street and hid behind a bush. They didn't have to wait long before the Honda returned.

Mike walked to the end of the driveway and lingered by his mailbox. He took his time, trying to look oblivious while sifting through the mail. He flinched subtly and grimaced with an attempt to remain calm as he eyed the Honda coming toward his house. It was going even faster than the first time around.

Carey held her hands over her son's ears after bringing him to the front seat of the Corolla.

A thin sheet of cold sweat formed on her back as she watched Ron aim carefully with his Glock. He rested the butt of the handgun on his left forearm and exhaled before he fired.

- - - - -

Mike Simmons nearly peed himself, but he instead ran as the Honda skipped into his driveway and slammed into his house. A bullet from Ron's Glock had torn through the driver's side front tire.

"Dammit!" Mike yelled as the car stopped upon slamming into his living room, far from Brian. He had stashed his son in the bathroom toward the rear of his two-story brick house. "I should kill you sons of bitches!"

He went bare-handed toward the Honda wreckage and tore the door away from the frame to see a Beretta .38 semiautomatic handgun staring back at him from the passenger's side. Mike froze when he saw the dead driver and the terminally wounded passenger pointing the Beretta. Fortunately for him, life left the passenger before he could squeeze the trigger.

Carey held John by the street as Ron followed Mike to retrieve Brian from the house. The three of them emerged two minutes later. Mike and Brian were bawling their eyes out as Ron led them toward the Corolla.

After checking to see that John was doing okay, Ron embraced Carey and kissed her fully on the lips. She completely disregarded the start of her shift at Hooters due to more immediate problems. There wasn't much time to process events as they jogged to Mike's garage so that that they could buy some time to evade the expected police response.

After Mike got Brian situated safely in the

back seat of his Jeep Grand Cherokee, he lent a set of keys to Lizzy's Saturn Astra to Ron and Carey to help them and her son blend in better. After making the car switch, Ron parked the Corolla down the street and joined Carey and John in the Saturn. All five of them headed back to Carey's apartment.

At the studio apartment, Brian and John played with Matchbox cars, smashing them together in the kitchenette while the adults talked in the small living space. Carey and Ron filled Mike in on what Ron had found out the last couple days through his trips to the library and observations gathered from businessmen, politicians, and men they'd killed or roughed-up to defend themselves.

"Nicholas Ferranti is a good match for the Sicilian Boss," Mike said in agreement. "Ferranti used to be an associate of Joey Lombardo, at least according to some references in the press. I saw correspondence to hint that my boss, Mayor Peck, is on the take from Ferranti."

Mike Simmons played with his iPhone for a good five minutes before returning his attention to Ron and Carey.

"I've forwarded texts with the Nokia phone number for the Sicilian Boss and our suspicions to an FBI buddy whom I've already contacted in Chicago. My guess is that if you two keep your heads low, I play dumb with the local police about the Honda running into my house, and we feed information to my FBI buddy, it'll throw off the mob assholes until the Feds do their jobs. We should keep to the background as the professionals take over."

"How are we gonna do that, Mike?" Ron asked. "Those assholes probably have your wife and will likely strike at you again. They've taken shots at Carey and I. I'm not one to lie down and wait things out. You can't do that during a firefight."

"I know that you have to keep a clear head when everyone else wants to panic," Mike responded. "Ferranti is trying to scare me. He'll shit his pants when he sees me do a press conference on TV to assure the public that I am well, unprovoked, and looking to serve our city. If Peck is as dirty as I think, he'll feel the heat as well."

Ron looked at Mike Simmons with a bit of respect and nodded.

"I won't go looking for trouble," he said, "but I'll kill whoever tries to hurt me, my friends, or the only surviving member of my family."

"I wouldn't expect any less," Mike said before he took Brian to continue on to City Hall. "I usually keep my Colt locked in my safe. But I'll be keeping it close to me while my son stays at a relative's house for the immediate future."

Carey hugged Mike goodbye before Ron shook his hand and they went their separate ways. The heat was on.

17

Revelations

Nicky Ferranti showed up at Hooters just after lunchtime on Tuesday. He had earlier called the manager and received quite a bit of deference from him. Ferranti could have on-the-house wings and beer as he observed all the waitresses. He waited for the manager to greet him and talk about a certain recent hire.

I'm tired of having to do everything myself, he thought. *What choice do I have when nearly all my help is incompetent? Thank God that the Chicago boys sent me a new driver and assistant at least. Drucci is superb.*

The manager interrupted with a pock-marked hand that stretched out from a navy blue polo shirt two sizes too big. Ferranti shook his limp grasp and read a name tag that said Richard as the manager introduced himself.

"I tell you I don't immediately recall a Carey Sullivan, but I usually don't focus on the names of my workers as a much as the way they work their assets, if you get my drift," Richard said before giving a monotone giggle. "I also don't recall any red heads, but I'll do what I can to help a fellow small business owner. Starlet's Alley is a classy joint. Go ahead and take a look around. One of my gals will set you up with on-the-house refreshments."

Fortunately for Ferranti, the late Paretti had stock photos of all of his dancers going back to his takeover of Starlet's Alley in 2004. He found the photograph of one Carey Sullivan, who started late into the summer of 2005, about six months after having a kid. Information on her kid or the father was unavailable, but he knew he was looking for a curvy, fit redhead with hazel eyes.

Unfortunately for his stakeout, none of the waitresses Ferranti saw working the shift were redheads. Also, the wings he had were not good, and the two Bud Lights he drank were likely watered down, so he didn't even get a mild buzz. He wanted to punch the manager after the tiresome troll didn't even recognize the face in the photos.

Ferranti asked his college-aged, brunette waitress to get Richard after he held a $5 bill above a well-proportioned cleavage next to a name tag that said Roxy. She took the bill and stuffed it in her bra before wagging her hips to the back of the restaurant. In a short while, the pock-marked perv was back at his side.

"I didn't see the girl I'm interested in," Ferranti said. "I'd be willing to pay good money to get one of my best dancers back. The sum would probably be more than she earns in two weeks here. You sure I can't take a took at personnel files?"

"Sir, even if we did keep as good of files as other businesses, the city pays us good subsidies to abide by all laws. Unless she's breaking a law herself or you are a cop, I'm afraid all of our employee files are off limits to private parties," Richard said. "More wings?"

Ferranti responded by forcefully knocking his empty beer glass off of the table. He swiftly elbowed Richard in the head when the manager tried to attend to the shards on the floor. Ferranti helped him up by the scruff of his neck.

"I have good friends with the Woolrich Public Health Department, Dick," he lied. "Flying glasses and these slick tabletops might be a problem for you if they feel the need to get involved. You ready to help me keep things clean and copacetic?"

A few other customers in the early afternoon grew nervous as the Richard gave a high-pitched whistle. The sound signaled waitstaff to flirt more aggressively and show more cleavage. It was usually reserved for times when the kitchen prepared several orders poorly, but this time, he used it to avoid further beatings.

"We had a waitress a no-show today. I think her name is Carey," Richard said after gesturing for Ferranti to follow his limp shuffle toward the back of the franchise. "Oh yeah, now I recognize the name. Her current address is near the Woolrich Walmart. So maybe there's apartments near there."

Ferranti slapped Richard on the back hard enough to not be friendly.

"Well then. Thanks for the watered-down beer and the tasteless wings, Dick," he said. "I'm sure city government won't find anything wrong. You've been most helpful."

After the manager regained his balance and gave a grim smile, Ferranti exited the Hooters and headed to his Lincoln. His new driver opened the door for him and they headed back toward Starlet's Alley with the tiny scrap of new information.

"Drucci," he said. "I'm feeling well for the first time in a while. Please make sure a Ketel One Martini greets me in my back office after we get back to Starlet's Alley. I need to watch the news for any mention of disruption to this small, pleasant community."

"As you wish, sir," Drucci replied.

He phoned ahead for the Martini on his Bluetooth before accelerating the Lincoln.

- - - - -

Ferranti entered Starlet's Alley and retreated to his back office. He was pleased that a freshly-shaken Ketel One martini greeted him at his desk. He clicked on the TV and Mike Simmons' seemingly placid face on a breaking WGN news update made him nervous. What Ferranti saw made him waste a gulp of his perfectly-made drink when he spit it against the wall.

"What the hell is going on?" he asked himself as the press conference of car crash near Simmons' home. "Why do my employees keep failing me?"

Mike Simmons addressed the cameras, saying that he and his son were safe despite the errant car near his house. No weapons were reported found at the scene of the crash. Woolrich police seemed to think that the driver and passenger of a Honda Accord had just been driving recklessly when an obstruction in the road punctured a tire. Toxicology results and names of the deceased were unavailable as of press time.

Before Mayor Peck could address the audience, Mike Simmons addressed speculation from a reporter about the whereabouts of his wife. He said he had no reason to believe that anything malicious had happened to her. He explained that Lizzy was likely attending to pressing family issues.

"I simply ask that my family's privacy be respected," he said. "We should instead focus on the issues voters hold most dear."

At least Simmons didn't do anything to cast suspicion the two incompetent goons, Ferranti thought. *But then again, why didn't he? He must have had help if they're dead...which reminds me of another one of my problems.*

Ferranti set up and snorted some cocaine from his desk. The rush to his sinuses didn't calm his unease as he called upon Gino Drucci.

"You've got other skills than driving," he said. "Carey Simmons and the asshole who've been giving us so much trouble, Ron McCallister, are at the apartments by the Walmart. I need a smart guy like you to go over there earlier tomorrow. I'm thinking a hostage might put them in an uncomfortable situation and they'd make a rash move. If you've got a good victim and a couple of thugs under your wing, we could flush them out."

After a few minutes, Drucci brought his hand from his hairless chin and spoke.

"Tomorrow I'll show up with three guys armed with Glock 18 automatics," he said. "Why don't you use Lizzy Simmons as a hostage? She's a high profile missing person and our targets would likely want to help her."

Ferranti ran a hand over the stubble on his cheek before he downed the rest of his martini and responded in a low voice. For once, he was hopeful that he had been handed competent help on a silver platter.

"That's why you'll go far, Drucci," he replied. "If Carey or her bouncer boyfriend see that one of their friends is in trouble, they'll be more likely to cooperate. Why don't you help yourself to one of the broads while you rest up for tomorrow? I'll get one of my other, less-qualified men to give me a ride home."

Drucci just smiled and bowed his head before responding.

"I'm just a humble servant that our friends in

Chicago chose to help expand business in Woolrich," he said. "Let me know if I can be of further assistance."

Ferranti smacked his lips, huffed a breath, and waved him off without further thought.

- - - - -

Since Anne De Silva had escaped from the Holiday Inn Express and bondsman Dan Jurecki, she kept to wooded areas and smoked the rest of her Virginia Slims. After her cigarettes were gone and hunger pangs set in, she called the number of the maid-of-honor from her wedding. Julia Ruben was the one person Anne could trust with everything and anything.

Anne had been staying with Julia, on the second floor of a three-flat a few miles west of Starlet's Alley, where the latter stripped most evenings. Julia didn't hesitate to help her friend. There was no issue sharing the 1970s-era, shag-rug, pink-walled, eight hundred square feet of living space.

Anne had just cleaned Jurecki's Sig Sauer and eaten a previously frozen pizza. She nearly destroyed a freshly-rolled joint when an image on WGN news struck her.

"What the hell is my baby wearing?" Anne said. "She looks like a cut-rate prostitute."

She dropped her joint when she saw her daughter in the audience of a press conference. Kendra looked thin, strung out, and like she hadn't showered for days.

"Oh yeah, I didn't recognize her from before," Julia said. "Kendra's changed her looks quite a bit since George got killed. She's been hanging around with some tough-looking grease balls at Starlet's Alley. I'm sorry I didn't recognize her earlier or I'd have told her to get in touch with her mother, for Christ's sake."

Anne had to calm her nerves. She got the joint she had dropped and nearly destroyed. She lit it, inhaled, and breathed out the sweet-smelling carcinogenic smoke before talking in an almost monotone, serious voice.

"When you get off work tonight, I'll be in the parking lot with the Taurus," she said. "All you have to do is get her near the car and I'll put her inside so we can get her back here and sorted out."

Julia shook her head, but maintained steady eye contact while responding.

"I'll do my damnedest to get her to come with me," she said. "I do a little blow from time to time so I'll offer her some candy to get her to the lot. I will help you get in touch with your daughter, toots. But we can't keep her here. The tough guys she's been hanging around have my address, probably have mob connections, and wouldn't hesitate to kill us all.""

Anne got up from the couch. She pulled her auburn hair into a pony tail before she paced from one end of the flat to the other. She took another generous hit of the joint before she spoke.

"I'll do what I have to do to get Kendra back," she said. "Just get her to the lot. I'll use drugs if I have to. I'll take her somewhere more safe, and you will have plausible deniability."

"What does that mean? Where will you go?"

Anne took another hit before responding.

"If I told you, you wouldn't be able to play innocent with cops, mobsters, or both when asked about my whereabouts or how you're involved. If anyone does ask about your actions, you can tell them that you were just trying to expand business for your boss. You'll have to get your own ride home though."

"That's no problem, hon. I'm on board. Once you get someplace safe, give me a ring after a week or so. I can get an occasional day off," Julie said.

Anne watched as her friend got on a plain white blouse over a red tube top that hugged her chest. Julia's boot-cut jeans and red lipstick were meant make any man stand to attention. The two hugged before Anne dropped Julia off to work at Starlet's Alley. They'd try to take Kendra from the club after Julia's shift.

- - - - -

Nicky Ferranti had another Glenlivet as he noticed the Tuesday night crowd thinning twenty minutes before midnight. Julia "Gonzagas" Ruben had just tossed her unbuttoned blouse toward three Japanese businessmen who remained glued to the stage. His eyes were wide open when she tore off her strapless bra and hip-hugging, black lace boy shorts. As the second to last act, she showed the remaining eight or so official customers every inch of her voluptuous but taut body. The only thing she wore was her three-inch ruby heels.

"Should I start selling candy, boss?" a musclebound bouncer with a crew cut asked. "I'd say that the rest of these jokers are waiting more for drugs than tits and ass. Well maybe not the Oriental businessmen; they probably don't see curves like that back in China."

Ferranti waved off Kendra, who had just done a line of blow off the table of his booth and was distracting him despite the fact that she was both underage and nuts. Ferranti gave the go-ahead with the wave of his hand, took the other dram of Glenlivet, and turned his attention to the muscle. He didn't pay attention as Kendra wandered to a back dressing room soon before Julia exited the stage.

"After the dancer that follows Gonzagas, we'll close up shop and start selling powder," he said. "The cop in the audience may be on our dole, but he's still a cop. Send Gonzagas his way to offer some complimentary services. She's got no more work tonight on stage."

The bouncer went in the back of Starlet's Alley to get Julia, but didn't return in the next several minutes. This agitated Ferranti when he saw Kendra and the dancer the bouncer had been sent to retrieve. The two women were giggling to themselves loudly and were heading hastily to the front entrance. Julia had re-sheathed herself in her tube top and jeans, and Kendra had a bloody fist.

Ferranti motioned for one of his bouncers with close-set eyes to keep his attention on the loud ladies. He signaled a bald-headed bouncer to join him and find out what had happened in the back.

When Ferranti stumbled into the back room, he punched the wall when he saw his crew cut bouncer crumpled unconscious on the floor with a knife sticking out of belly. He ordered the bald bouncer call the one with close-set eyes. They were both to follow Julia and Kendra and take them by force. Ferranti cocked his Ruger .44 semiautomatic handgun and went to the front entrance to supervise the action.

"I'll get those bitches," Ferranti said to himself in a growling voice.

- - - - -

Anne De Silva pulled the maroon Ford Taurus near the front entrance to meet her friend and

141

her daughter as they came out of Starlet's Alley around midnight. She couldn't do anything, however, to stop a bouncer with close-set eyes from tackling Kendra to the ground ten yards away. Just after Anne erupted from the car, Ferranti burst outside and put two quick rounds into Julia's lower back.

There wasn't time to consider her friend's condition before Anne trained the Sig Sauer on the bastard who shot Julia. She screamed for him to order his goon release her daughter after firing near his left foot. She then trained the handgun on his groin to make the point that she should be obeyed.

The goofy-eyed bouncer released Kendra. Unfortunately for Anne, her daughter was freaking out too much to be coaxed into the Taurus. Kendra ran away from her mother, ducking behind a Ford Expedition. Anne swore loudly at the sky as she eased her grip on the Sig Sauer. Her eyes followed her daughter.

Ferranti took advantage of Anne's diverted attentions. He put a round through her shoulder, and the Sig Sauer dropped to the ground. The bald bouncer focused on Anne and swiftly shot her in the chest. This was something that Ferranti did not want.

He wasted no time in putting a round into the bald bouncer's forehead. The dead henchman had just mortally wounded a potentially valuable hostage.

Ferranti spit on the gravel ground in disgust and went over to Kendra. He offered her an arm to give her the illusion of trust. Instead of helping her stand, he punched her in the abs and ordered his remaining bouncer to take her to the trailer behind Starlet's Alley. She was to be subdued, but not roughed up.

Everyone who was in the parking lot made themselves scarce. Ferranti slowly shuffled back into the club. The rush of adrenaline and chemical euphoria gave him hastily-conceived ideas on how to handle hindrances to his success in the suburban scene. He was quite proud of himself when he rejoined his still-standing bouncer and Gino Drucci in the back office to present his plans. He had to take a deep breath to slow down.

"While you, Drucci, and three well-armed men try to flush out Carey and Ron tomorrow, I'm gonna take care of the Mike Simmons problem. I'm sick of screwing with the local bureaucrats. I add healthy bonuses to some of their salaries. They should see what happens to those who don't play ball."

Anyone who was listening maintained silence as Ferranti talked. Only Drucci dared to show a difference of opinion.

"Your ideas could prove more incendiary than insightful, sir," he said. "I would advise more caution if we want to keep things copacetic–."

"Shut up and do what you're told, Drucci!" Ferranti interrupted loudly. "Cocaine distribution in this shitty little suburb relies on my skillful stewardship. It'll be frustrating enough if my employees question things more than the locals."

Drucci just nodded his heated head and kept his mouth shut. There was still a lot going on behind his well-groomed, seemingly placid face.

"First, goofy-eyes here will have to put the former first lady, Gonzagas, and that bald-headed bastard under the ground in Lisle. Drucci, you follow to help bury our problems and pick up Lizzy to help you flush out our rats tomorrow. I'll call Chicago for reinforcements, which shouldn't be a problem."

A grin lit up Drucci's face before he joined the bouncer to carry out orders.

Ferranti commanded one of his strippers to service the crooked cop who said he "may or may not" have witnessed a parking lot disturbance. With the extra perks, the Woolrich police blotter didn't mention gunshots, stabbings, and deaths. Officially, it had been a typical Tuesday evening at Starlet's Alley. Anyone who could contradict that narrative was either dead, paid off, or a puppet for the interests of the Chicago mob.

18

Hitting Home

Carey was tending to John in her studio apartment's small living space when Ron noticed two silver Lincolns pulling into the parking lot of her apartment building late Wednesday morning. Carey hadn't ventured to work at Hooters in since her last shift on Sunday. Ron and she rightfully figured that whoever was looking for them would be watching any of their usual destinations.

I figured it would only be a matter of time until thugs from the mob or local police found out where we are staying, Ron thought. *Looks like those mob meatheads are more resourceful than expected.*

He shushed his roommates as he kept an eye on a stern-looking, olive-skinned man who exited one of the vehicles with a coked-up Lizzy Simmons while the driver remained inside. Unlike the three goons who exited from the other Lincoln, the one who held Lizzy walked as if he had rehearsed for Project Runway. He was clean-shaven and had an almost classy look about him despite holding a woman hostage in a parking lot.

Ron wanted to get Lizzy back for a reunion with her husband and son. He also hoped to not get arrested or killed. He considered taking the offensive before the thugs holding her hostage had a chance to strike.

These assholes really don't do subtlety, he thought. *That's a good thing for us.*

The clean-shaven captor, who had a blood-stemming grip on Lizzy's bicep, walked with a squint-eyed, cautious look on his face toward the apartment building. The other three gunmen had the cautiousness of truckers in a porn store. None of their guns were visible, but Ron could see conspicuous bulges in their coats.

Ron also thought about the situation in which he and Carey would find themselves if a few mobsters were killed outside the entrance to Carey's apartment building. Ubiquitous crime coverage near a Walmart was something that even insiders like Mike Simmons couldn't keep on the down low.

What if they don't find any bodies here? Ron asked himself. I am sick of racking up dead bodies, let alone with being stuck having to transport them in the Simmons family's Saturn.

He called Carey over to the window to see the trouble that they were in. He preemptively put a hand on her shoulder before she recognized her friend being led by the four thugs.

"Sons of bitches! They are taking a big risk," she said before taking a breath and regaining some composure to deal with the situation. "With her husband connected with the mayor, they must be–"

"Desperate, well-connected, or both," Ron said, completing the thought. "I have to add that they've got a lot of *cojones*, but we still have the upper hand since we are on home turf."

"Shooting goons in broad daylight is sure to be a media shit-show," Carey said. "But we gotta help Lizzy however we can."

Ron gently took her chin and gave her a kiss on the lips.

"I'll lead them somewhere where Lizzy's husband can claim self-defense if shots get fired," he said.

She returned his gaze and nodded, raising her right eyebrow.

"I know," he said. "It's not just about me."

She managed a quick wink as a show of confidence.

Ron quickly put on his windbreaker and White Sox cap. He stuffed in socks to make his belly look bigger and hide his fully-loaded Glock. He gave Carey a nod, returned the wink, and asked her to stay put he headed out the door and down the stairs.

In the parking lot with the mobsters approaching, he whistled a tune and walked opposite them toward the Walmart. He circled around back to the apartment lot when he realized their attentions were still on the building. He ran up on the far north side of the lot toward the Lincolns. He hoped that they were single-minded enough that they weren't paying any attention to him.

The four thugs took out cigarettes and wandered in front of the apartment building. They initially tried to look casual for two renters who exited the building separately. However, that was tough when you held a terrified, drugged hostage and stood together like frat boys looking to pillage a college freshman's house party. They soon decided to go "balls to the wall." The leader pulled a Glock automatic on Lizzy.

Ron made his move. He stalked toward the back of the empty Lincoln. He stabbed the remaining two cheap steak knives into its back wheels before he crept up the Lincoln Lizzy had arrived in. The stout driver inside was dutifully keeping watch over the other four goons and their hostage.

The driver gave a wide-eyed look of surprise when his door opened. Ron gave him a nonlethal blow to the throat to keep him quiet and followed with a blow to the temple to knock him out. Ron had some difficulty moving the corpulent driver to the passenger's seat of the car. He didn't take the time to enjoy the looks on the four thugs faces when he started the car, shot out the windshield of the other Lincoln and sped off toward the Simmons household.

- - - - -

Carey had to stifle her worry as she watched the lead hostage-taker and two of his goons jog with Lizzy toward the empty Lincoln to pursue Ron. One of the four thugs stayed behind to pick up any slack. She put John on her twin mattress before she retrieved the other Glock 9 mm semiautomatic from above her kitchenette sink, turned off the safety, chambered a round, and put in a fresh clip. She gave John a kiss on the forehead and told him to stay put before leaving.

After going down the stairs, she skulked outside and toward the back o a dumpster to remain unnoticed by the remaining gunman. She noticed he was exponentially more agitated than before with his jerky movements and a twitching eye. In his right hand, he gripped what appeared to an automatic handgun with a large magazine.

Fortunately for her, his lack of subtlety and the car chase left her apartment parking lot devoid of any witnesses. Unfortunately for them both, he noticed her and brought up his arms to aim at her. She didn't give him a chance to use his automatic as she carefully took aim and shot him in the chest with two shots from her Glock.

After taking out the remaining hostile, Carey rushed back upstairs to her apartment and locked the deadbolt. She called Mike Simmons on his cell phone to warn him that trouble might be headed his way. He informed her that he'd call police and not to worry. Her mind was the opposite of calm, but she forced herself to pretend otherwise for John's sake.

She returned the Glock to its place above the sink, bent down near the mattress, and pulled John into her arms. She waited for any developments to be broadcast over WGN radio. John simply bashed two of his Matchbox cars together. He made explosion sounds while he rested calmly in his mother's lap.

- - - - -

Ron hadn't had a chance to tell Mike Simmons that he was being tailed by his wife and some of the goons who had held her hostage in front of Carey's apartment. For one thing, he hated to talk on his cell phone while driving. For another thing, he was being aggressively chased by angry mobsters. The Lincoln in pursuit was cruising along despite any leaked air from its tires.

It turns out that someone has called ahead, Ron thought as he saw two police cruisers, their lights flashing, in front of the Simmons' house. He decided to turn on a dime down a parallel street to the East. Fortunately for him, the mobsters didn't have as much control as they went toward the Simmons household. They stopped just before they hit a cruiser.

When Ron stopped about a quarter mile away from the scene, he realized that he had received two texts. One was from Carey, telling him about contacting Simmons. An earlier one was from Simmons.

It read:

I stopped giving information to my FBI friend when a mob boss called from prison and offered my wife's return if I could stay under the radar. I urged my FBI friend to get in touch with you and Carey. With his help, you should do fine.

"Asshole," Ron said to his phone. "Don't think that getting out of a fight with murderers, drug dealers, and assassins will help you protect the ones you love or clear your conscience."

Jesus, did I just say that? Ron asked himself as he tried to drive casually toward Highway 34. *I think Aunt Peggy's high expectations of humanity are rubbing off on me.*

As Ron passed the street where the police cruisers were mulling around Mike Simmons' home, a huge explosion lit up the house and anyone inside it. Flames leaped out, causing cops to flea before their cruisers could become engulfed. A barely-functioning Lincoln putted away from the scene while officers dialed for backup.

Ron didn't stop and get any more information before he gunned the stolen Lincoln toward the highway. His thoughts ran at an explosive speed. He didn't watch out for a tail. He just hoped to get back to Carey and John. Moreover, he hoped he would get back to them in enough time to help them stay alive.

- - - - -

Carey shut off the radio after finding out from a breaking news update that part of the block where the Simmons family had lived was in flames. No one had yet reported about the shooting in her parking lot. She wasn't displeased at the lack of attention, but she was uneasy, to say the least.

She grabbed a duffel bag lying near her

mattress and put the clips of recovered 9 mm
ammunition inside. Her Glock was loaded and
primed to fire, and she put it in her sweatshirt
pocket with the safety engaged. She added to
the bag a six-pack of Mott's applesauce cups,
one of Ron's black t-shirts, a change of clothes
for her and John, and other basic supplies her
three-year-old would need for the next week. She
soon crept downstairs and to the side door of the
apartment building with her son.

Oh, this is just stupidly brilliant, she thought
as she saw a police cruiser containing two
officers sitting next to the Saturn. *Where the hell
were you when mobsters were holding my friend
hostage? Shit, I hope Lizzy's still alive.*

Carey put John and the duffel bag just inside
the door to the building as she made her move.
She ruffled her dark red hair, unbuttoned the
first three buttons of her blouse, and unzipped
her sweatshirt to give a more than generous
view of her cleavage. The cops didn't look at her
face when she joined them. She also adopted a
Minnesota accent, not looking for subtlety.

"Oh, hey there, officers," she said to the cop
on the driver's side, holding her face above the
roof of the car so they'd focus on other things. "I
just saw some lady takin' her kid and some other
guy toward the Walmart. I think I saw one of 'em
shoot at some boys in a Lincoln. Here's my
number if you guys need more information to
make an arrest. I just hate law-breakers looking
to bring down the neighborhood, ya know?"

Carey handed them the home phone number
of the Hooters manager as she strutted north in
the opposite direction of John. As the officers
headed to Walmart, she retraced a path to get
John and their supplies. She and her son went

back to the Saturn Astra before making their way toward Highway 34. She tried to get a hold of Ron, calling at stoplights. Her eyes lit up and her lips curved into a smile when he finally answered.

- - - - -

Mayor Peck sipped a double latte in the back of his red BMW while being driven to the office later in the afternoon. He was angry that he wasn't able to run on his treadmill before taking lunch. Also, his wife had refused sex earlier in the morning. It didn't improve his mood that he had to address reporters about the recent death of the man he had hired to deal with them. The mob was being less than cooperative.

Goddammit, I'm still the head of Woolrich, Peck thought. *I'll cover for the deaths of a couple of lowlifes and let mobsters deal drugs at Starlet's Alley, but Mike was my legitimate line to the locals. Ferranti is keeping his affairs decidedly not copacetic with the community.*

Mayor Peck took the microphone as cameras from WGN and the local Fox affiliate focused on him standing behind a podium. His wife stood to his right in front of the flags of the United States and Illinois. He appeared calm despite the internal buzzing of his thoughts. He delivered part of what Ferranti had faxed directly to his office half an hour prior to the press conference.

"Fellow citizens of Woolrich, it is with great sorrow that I announce the death of my Communications Director Mike Simmons. Immediate investigators at the scene are looking into the possibility that the explosion resulted from a broken gas pipeline underground. Also, the whereabouts of Mike Simmons' wife, Elizabeth, are still unknown."

Rob Peck deviated here on from his approved script. He wanted to push back a little on his illicit business partners

"We believe that Mrs. Simmons would show up at City Hall if she knew what happened. We will hold a funeral service this Saturday. Two Woolrich police officers will be tasked with getting in touch with her and escorting her to the memorial if she so wishes," Peck said. "May you feel safe that our finest law enforcement is on the job. God bless you all."

A flood of questions hit the mayor as he went to his wife and left the podium. Fox wanted to know more about the cause of the explosion. WGN wanted to know about rumors that Mike Simmons' wife was actually dead. No one irked him as much as the two musclebound gentlemen sulking outside of a black Lincoln. He pretended not to see them.

Five minutes later in the BMW, Mayor Peck received a call on his cell phone from the Metropolitan Correctional Center. Against his better judgment, Peck ignored the call and deleted the voicemail before he had a chance to listen to it. The mayor sent a police cruiser to monitor Starlet's Alley and asked his bodyguard to remain more vigilant than usual.

After Peck returned to his home, he didn't notice any of Ferranti's patrol around his block. He was instead finding release by having sex with his wife. The exercise was intended to calm his nerves, but it was also because he felt an urge to take advantage of someone other than the Woolrich general public.

Mayor Peck got off and finished the session with his wife. After the ten minutes "cuddle time" required of him, he locked himself in his home office with the remainder of a fifth of Tito's vodka. He looked at the WGN news website on his Toshiba laptop while considering his next move.

It's time to ask the mob for money, he thought. *I've got friends in higher levels of "law enforcement" who can strike harder than any mobster. Dammit, I'll always be relevant.*

Just then, his wife knocked on he door and announced that there was call from a Mr. Lombardo. Peck couldn't ignore it.

19

Runaway

Ron McCallister woke up Thursday morning in a 1997 Pontiac Grand Am that was parked in a junkyard. He was in the front seat while Carey was in the back seat with John on her lap. She interrupted a breakfast of applesauce to give Ron a brief kiss on his still sleepy cheek.

It took him a few minutes to remember how they had gotten to the Grand Am. After the Simmons household exploded, he was driving in the stolen Lincoln on Highway 34 when he noticed a police checkpoint at the exit to get to Carey's apartment. He pulled to the side of the highway over a half mile before the exit and called her.

Ron told her that the exit was swarming with police and gave her his location. While she drove to a frontage road parallel to the highway, he wiped his prints off of the steering wheel, turn signal, shifter, and door handle of the Lincoln. He took the money from the wallet of the portly driver still unconscious in the passenger's seat. He hopped the dividing fence to the frontage road and joined Carey and John in the Saturn. From there, she drove them to the junkyard where they currently hid on the edge of Woolrich. They took the back roads to avoid police and left the fingerprint-wiped Saturn in a ditch about a half mile from where they currently were.

In the Grand Am, he took a quick inventory before he and his fellow outlaws could figure out the next step. He still had the Nokia with the mobsters' numbers, his Glock, and his Samsung. Carey still had her Motorola, her Glock, and some extra clips of 9 mm ammo. They had about $450 cash from the past week.

I could really go for a pull of Jack, he thought, running his right hand through his unkempt black-dyed hair and mangy beard. *But I gotta keep it together for the doll and her cute kid in the back seat.*

Ron hoped Simmons had really given his information to his friend in the FBI. If his friend wasn't dirty, it was probably the only way that the three of them would have any peace within the foreseeable future. The Grand Am lacked the wheels to make it otherwise more useful than mere shelter from the elements.

"Well gorgeous, the closest gas station is about a mile from here," he finally said to Carey. "If you and the little man stay put, I'll see about some transport and any news about the manhunt. I'm sorry toots, but right now it's just us against the mob and the local police. If Mike's friend in the FBI is legit, we may get some backup."

From the rearview mirror, he watched as her peach-colored lips gave a smile that radiated despite their situation. The sight stirred his stomach in a sentiment that he thought of as hopeful.

"I've still got my men, and you told me you saw Lizzy alive after I picked you up," she said. "Let's try to focus on the positive, handsome. John is looking for us to lead here."

"I never thought I'd say this, but I hope that the Feds will put their resources to work and give us a hand," he said before giving her and John a grin meant to be reassuring.

Ron blew her a kiss and gave the kid a wink before he exited the car. He crept out of the junkyard toward what some may consider civilization. When he saw the occasional, random car, he kept his face pointed toward the ground, happy that he had remembered his White Sox cap. He tried to maintain a brisk, yet casual pace.

- - - - -

Before entering the Shell gas station about a mile or so down the road, Ron kept the brim of his hat low in hopes the clerk would have less of a reason to identify him. He picked up and paid for a *Naperville Sun*, a coffee, some travel cereal boxes, string cheese, beef jerky, and bottled water. He exited the gas station with no worries about recognition from the bored, long-haired, high school-aged clerk.

The *Sun* confirmed his fears about Mike Simmons from the front page headline. He was pleased after skimming further during his walk that the media speculated that the explosion didn't result from a problem with the gas pipeline. Thoughts stewed in his head as he took a convoluted path along several roads.

He figured that the mob would be pissed off about any added investigation into their business at Starlet's Alley. He hadn't expected any additional pressure on them from Mayor Peck, but that's what the *Sun* reported. A thunderous crash near the road to the junkyard interrupted whatever was going on in his head.

Ron flinched as he saw that a Jeep Wrangler had just run a Honda Civic to the shoulder The driver and passenger of the Wrangler jumped out and ran towards the Civic. Both were armed with handguns.

There's both duty and opportunity here, he thought.

Ron didn't want to commit larceny against some civilians simply trying to make it through the day, but he welcomed the chance to take a Jeep from some thugs attempting armed robbery. He put down the plastic bag containing the contents of his latest shopping trip before he stealthily dashed toward the scene.

"Don't move," the Jeep driver yelled, holding his handgun toward the man in the driver's seat of the Civic. "My partner will have no problem killing your woman or your kid."

The partner was about to pull a handgun on the lady in the passenger's seat, but was stopped when a 9 mm bullet from a Glock tore through his kneecap. The assailant with the gun that had been pointed at the Civic driver dropped his weapon and emptied his bladder when Ron put his head in the line of fire from about fifteen yards away.

"Hit the ground, take off your pants, and put your hands behind your heads," Ron told them. The robbers did as told while the couple in the Civic looked on incredulously. The child in the back seat was curiously calm.

Ron took the would-be robbers' wallets from their pants after he had kicked away their guns. He pocketed $150 for himself and handed $150 to the couple in the Civic. He also took the keys to the Jeep and the two thugs' IDs. He tossed their pants to the other side of the road.

"You guys picked the wrong day and time to commit a robbery," Ron said before knocking them each out with a kick to the head. He said to the couple in the Civic: "You people be careful, forget you saw me, have a good day, and watch out for bandits. There's a lot of psychos out there."

The Civic driver and his passengers nodded their heads. The man gave Ron a wave and a smile before they headed toward the Shell gas station. Ron retrieved his jerky, his other refreshments, and his newspaper in the bag before taking the Jeep the other direction.

He parked the Jeep on the road a few blocks from the junkyard to maintain some anonymity before walking the rest of the way to John and Carey. After a few minutes of explanation, he brought their food, weapons, and other supplies from the Grand Am. Carey carried John to the new ride.

20

Party Time

Nicky Ferranti finished a line of cocaine off of a sensuously sedated stripper's bare shoulder before he contacted a Naperville florist to order white carnations and lilies for Mike Simmons' funeral. It was Thursday evening at Starlet's Alley, and he decided to feel good despite not being able to kill Carey nor Ron. He also had to deal with a less than pliant mayor, who, according to his top man, Drucci, wanted either more payoff or action to keep things copacetic. He made sure he had plenty of Glenlivet to drink while he told himself that he was the one in charge of Woolrich.

That's not to say that the extra police presence didn't rattle him.

Ferranti also watched for any reaction on Kendra's part about Tuesday evening's events. She didn't even seem to realize that her mother, Anne, had died. Perhaps she was just acting oblivious despite her experience. He decided to not focus on those worries when she snorted a line off his table.

To his chagrin, he hadn't been able to do as many cocaine sales since Mayor Peck had decided to keep watch on Starlet's Alley. He'd only been able to sell between four and five in the morning when the police changed shifts. He figured that blowing up Mike Simmons was overkill brought on by an adrenaline-fueled bender, but an inside source said the asshole had called the FBI on him. This helped Ferranti rationalize the move.

The local rent-a-cops will likely call off their

dogs after the flowers arrive for the funeral, he thought. *My deepest condolences should help. Lizzy won't be available to contradict my intentions.*

The Simmons widow was currently in shorts and a tank top borrowed from one of the strippers. She was blasted out of her mind and handcuffed in the late Sal Paretti's trailer, acting as a guinea pig for a new source of cocaine that Ferranti wanted to introduce for his more professional clientele. Businessmen, aldermen, and other more respectable junkies had higher expectations after all.

Lizzy's lack of clothes made it harder for her to escape her situation, and Ferranti liked the look. He didn't risk pimping her out to corrupt cops or drunkards after bar time. The woman still had a self-defense streak in her. Even with her hands cuffed, she kicked the crap out of a bouncer the other night when the idiot tried to make a lecherous move.

Still, if she ever gets a bit more tame, she could be a star, Ferranti thought. *The customers like the girls with more curves. I might have to ease her off the candy since she's starting to look more like Kate Moss than Kate Winslet.*

As a blonde stripper, who had been wearing a pink camisole with "Princess" sequined across her D-cup breasts, stepped down from the stage, Ferranti beckoned her toward his booth. It was nearing prime time at the club and he needed to relax, get a somewhat decent sleep, and take a day before having to put on a polite face for Saturday's funeral.

"What do you say, toots?" Ferranti asked the blonde. "You want to make a relaxed man out of me for $200 an hour? You can spend the night at my house, but I don't pay you to sleep. I don't have to warn you about what will happen if you try and rip me off."

He and the blonde went to Drucci, who was commanded to drive them to Ferranti's greystone house. Once the Lincoln pulled up, Drucci dutifully cased the place before they entered. Drucci poured them drinks and delivered them to a hot tub in Ferranti's four hundred square foot bedroom.

The blonde didn't get through more than half of her Cosmopolitan before Ferranti finished his Glenlivet and ordered her to please him. After a couple hours in the Jacuzzi, he ordered her to towel him off before she sensuously sauntered to the bed and beckoned him with a slender, nimble finger. She got him off and massaged his shoulders before he slipped into a deep sleep and she could finally relax.

She flipped on the TV in an adjacent room and lit a joint. She watched the Home Shopping Network with apathetic greed for a while before falling asleep on the couch where she sat. Drucci called a cab for her later in the morning. He then woke Ferranti and prepared breakfast with fresh espresso.

- - - - -

Carey Sullivan woke up Friday just before nine a.m. in the queen-sized bed she shared with her son at a Travelodge in Naperville. They had checked in yesterday evening, arriving in their new Jeep. She payed $320 in cash and used her fake ID to reserve a week so that they could all lie low. Thankfully, the Jeep came with nearly a full tank of gas, they had enough supplies for a week, and they had over $150 cash remaining. The complimentary breakfast and coffee was a bonus, even if wasn't half as good as what Ron could make on a simple stove top.

After she meandered her way to the breakfast area, Carey made herself a waffle on the self-service machine before snagging a plate full of bacon for herself and her boys. She swiped extra muffins, bananas, juice, whole milk, and bagels before the cut-off time for breakfast. She relaxed with her food, a cup of coffee and CNN in the lobby. She planned to return within the hour to her sleeping son and a man with whom she'd never been so close.

Carey wondered why they hadn't become friends before thugs resolved to target them for death. Given the amount that they had both improvised and fought to survive the last week or so, she had to think positively about what they could accomplish if they returned to everyday life, where they didn't have to run from law enforcement and the mob. The thugs had been reliably incompetent, but they were still a buzz kill.

We wouldn't be the yuppie, upper class that votes for assholes like Peck or De Silva or donates large sums of money to our church, she thought. *But we wouldn't return to our lives as a stripper and a bouncer at a sleazy strip club. There's got to be a middle ground somewhere.*

She kept her mind in the present when she returned to the room, opened the door, and gently tended to John.

"What time is it?" Ron asked after he awoke from his slumber in the other bed. He took a sip of his black coffee and gave a deep groan that she had come to enjoy. "You can wake me up anytime if you bring back breakfast. Hell, I might wake your ass up if I was the one to bring back food and coffee."

"I wanted to let the boys nestle in their beds a bit longer," Carey replied as she gave a blueberry muffin and milk for her son. "There's no sense in waking a three-year-old and a grumpy man when I can have a few minutes to myself. Besides, John can can take care of himself when I leave him alone for a bit. Can't you?"

John smiled to them while she tossed Ron a copy of the *Naperville Sun*. It was another useful amenity of their motel. He gave her a cheeky chuckle and thanked her for the coffee while grabbing some of the breakfast.

He read, sipping substandard coffee and eating bacon. She gave John an orange juice before she fixed another coffee for herself with cream and Splenda. She interrupted him when she noticed something on the reverse side of the newspaper.

"Shit! It'll be hard to get to Mike's funeral tomorrow," Carey said, excusing herself for her language in front of John. "By the way, whenever the FBI gets in contact with us and sanctions it, I'd like to visit Ferranti and all the other lowlifes at Starlet's Alley. One of those evil dicks knows where Lizzy is. There's a number of other women there who should learn something about castration."

"Yes, ma'am," Ron said, defensively covering his package. "I'll see if we can't speed along the process, with or without the authorities."

The look of retribution toward the thugs responsible didn't leave Carey's face even as Ron helped her clean the room from breakfast and their slumber the night before. Ron grew a bit more relaxed as his roommate kissed him on the cheek.

"Well, I'm happy we all got time now when we don't have to shoot at bandits or steal from them," Carey said.

He grasped her shoulder before embracing her and meeting her lips with his. She gave him a deep hug and a smack on the behind before he left the room to get some space. She soon joined her son on the floor and played with crumpled newspaper while Ron brooded in the lobby and drank motel coffee.

- - - - -

Ron wanted to write to his Aunt Peggy and explain how he felt about her, Carey, and John, whom she had met Monday. He wanted to apologize for not being able to show up for his weekly visit, even though he knew that she understood. He used the complimentary Travelodge stationary and pen before crumpling up letter after letter and dropping it in the waste basket.

He doubted he would have the chance to see her and didn't want to draw any unwanted attention to her because of his problems with the law. He drew some strength from the knowledge that he finally introduced Aunt Peggy to a nice gal and her son. He believed Carey when she said they'd had laughs during their visit.

Just as Ron began his walk back to the room he shared with the Sullivans, his Samsung rang. He flipped it open and gave a generic greeting with only his last name. He returned to the room he shared with Carey and John while listening to the voice coming out of the receiver.

"Ron McCallister, you need to meet me alone in the women's apparel department at the Woolrich Walmart in four hours," said a confident, baritone voice. "I'm with the FBI. I'll be wearing a navy blue down vest with a noticeable bulge in my chest to suggest a shoulder-holstered Glock semiautomatic. If I find that you are armed yourself, I have a sniper who can take you down if you provoke anything. So what do you say? Show us who you are, don't make us feel threatened, and we might me able to help you. Screw with us, and we will be obligated to return the favor."

Ron gently shushed for quiet when he returned to the room. He wanted to express cockiness over cooperation, even though the cards were not in his favor.

"Apart from threats to my health," Ron asked, "what can you do to instill a sense of trust in a tax-paying, law-abiding citizen who's only defending himself and those he doesn't want to see harmed?"

"Well, let's see, Mr. McCallister," the voice said. "You and the people you're presumably protecting were living at an apartment building across from the Walmart as of Wednesday. You saw our contact, Mike Simmons, a good friend of mine, get blown up. You, Ms. Sullivan, and her son are hiding out at the Travelodge off of Highway 34 in Naperville. I could visit you out there, but I figured that you would appreciate a more subtle approach."

Ron held the phone as if his hand had turned into a vise-grip. He decided to respond with a confidence that he didn't have.

"Well, I suppose I'm still the one who knows who you're after," Ron said. "If that isn't enough, you'll pay attention to the fact that I only give a damn about the people staying with me in Naperville. Your life is as immaterial to me as any mob asshole when it comes down to it. I'll see you in the women's section."

He hung up and explained the rough conversation on the phone to Carey before he washed his face and trimmed his beard to look slightly more respectable. They packed most of their belongings in the Jeep. They left the Nokia in a motel safe before making the trip to the Walmart. Once there, she dropped him off.

"If you see trouble, camp out somewhere off Highway 34," Ron said after he got out of the Jeep. "They know we are at the Travelodge. I'll find you two and we'll get a different place to hide out if these fellas have bad intentions."

They blew kisses at each other and John waved before he and Carey went down the road. Carey worried about whether she would hear good news from Ron or read about his death or arrest in the newspaper.

21

Ron and the Feds

FBI Agent Matt Russo thumbed through packages of Hanes boy short style panties at Walmart around four hours after Ron McCallister had hung up on him. While having to follow leads from his own investigation into organize crime in Woolrich's, his wife, Clara, wanted him to pick up something "cute" for her before returning to their Chicago residence. She was making steaks for their date night, and their six-year-old daughter, Zoe, was staying with a friend for the evening.

Russo had been looking forward to a night with his wife but had more than an inkling that duty would make him put it off. His investigation was picking up steam with possible witnesses to mob crimes.

The bureaucrats have been on our asses for supposedly being less efficient, Russo thought, picturing the face of his ass-kissing boss, Special Agent in Charge Dave Holbert. *So I gotta multitask to keep the wife and our pencil-pushing friends happy. Clara understands my job is important and sometimes duty calls. That's part of why I love her.*

Just as Russo remembered what size to get, he saw Ron out of his left eye. Ron had changed his appearance somewhat from the mugshot and Army veteran files from the FBI's Data Integration and Visualization System. He had dyed his hair black and had a neatly-trimmed beard with streaks of gray.

Russo pushed aside any professional frustrations and thoughts of his wife that would interfere with his duty on the ground. He ran his left hand through the pitch-black crew cut above his oval, olive-skinned face. The faint stubble on his chin matched his prickly perspective.

"Mr. McCallister, keep your hands where I can see them," he said after approaching Ron with long, quick strides. "I don't see Carey Sullivan or her kid here. So, you got the first part right. But what the hell is that in your front pocket?"

"You brought your Glock, so I brought mine," Ron said after giving a smirk. "When strangers call me up and threaten me, I usually carry a weapon, even if I don't want to use it. You can take it if you call your sniper off. I saw the shooter in the sporting goods department. You Feds might need to work on being more subtle."

"You let me take your Glock first," Russo said. "You can't get anything good done if you present a threat around a selection of discount women's intimates. By the way, my sniper's extremely accurate with his Special Police Rifle and has no collateral damage on his record."

A middle-aged, brunette woman with a bad perm across the aisle from them nearly fainted when she saw Ron allow Russo to take the Glock 9 mm semiautomatic. The agent shushed her and showed his badge. He then touched his right ear and told the sniper to stand down.

In another show of good faith, Russo showed Ron the depressed safety on his Glock .40 semiautomatic before he brought his subject along to buy the undergarments and leave the store. The agent and his sniper back up peacefully escorted Ron to a black Ford Expedition.

Agent Russo then collected Ron's Samsung, inspecting it and the call log before the sniper covered Ron's eyes with a blindfold. The Ford Expedition eventually reached a small, dilapidated-looking shack in a sparsely-populated area off of Highway 55.

"Welcome to the Bolingbrook interrogation office," Russo said as he removed the blindfold. The darkness of evening was beginning to creep over the sky.

"As we get to know each other better, we may make things more or less comfortable for you. We have to make sure you'll play ball and won't be a threat to our mutual safety."

Russo led Ron to the shack, with his driver and sniper partner soon joining them. A syringe full of clear liquid was shot into their captive's left deltoid muscle. They waited as Ron grew more sedate and candid. It wasn't as if he had a chance of escape even if he wasn't drugged. The driver even secured his hands behind his back with handcuffs.

The Chicago pencil-pushers and bean-counters would approve of truth serum, Russo thought. *I better call Clara about a rain check – again. She's really a saint.*

- - - - -

A dusty, cramped room appeared in front of Ron's eyes, becoming less blurry by the second. He began to feel nauseated with the movement of the room, but then he realized that his head was swaying, not the room. He tried to stand up, but hands rather forcefully held him down.

I not only feel stupid, but I probably look it too. My body won't respond to my nerves, Ron thought as he remembered his hands were cuffed behind a pole in the middle of the shack. *I don't want to make myself look more desperate by struggling against stainless steel.*

Agent Russo gave Ron a rather hard slap to the face. Ron felt blood or drool go down the right side of his chin. He hoped to hell that it was blood. He didn't want to look like a complete idiot. He looked up at Russo and the other two taxpayer-funded thugs. Their faces were dimly lit by a 60-watt incandescent bulb hanging from the ceiling. No light showed through the windows.

"I had hoped that you would have a Nokia on you with the names and contact info of mobsters collaborating with Mayor Rob Peck," Russo said. "We saw a couple of suspicious-looking goombahs tailing Peck at a press conference the other day. Peck may not care to find Lizzy Simmons, but I assure you, if you give us the Nokia and any other information that will help, the FBI is a great resource, My colleagues and I will help Ms. Simmons, Ms. Sullivan, and you get back to a normal life more quickly than anyone else."

Ron realized that Russo was probably in a rush because he was spilling information and bargaining much too early for someone who's job it was to play hardball. And though the FBI might be slightly more trustworthy than the Chicago mob, he wasn't yet willing to fully reveal his hand. Carey was still waiting for word from him that he was okay. A compulsion kept him from lying outright.

"Could the Nokia be lost or maybe have blown up in the explosion at Mike Simmons' house?" Ron asked with a wry smile. He figured answering an interrogation with questions was the most feasible way to obfuscate. "I noticed that one of the numbers came from Woolrich City Hall. What about trying there?"

Russo mopped up some of the blood on Ron's

chin before pressing what smelled like rubbing alcohol to his face. Ron tried to hide any reaction to the searing pain when the liquid stung a cut.

"Mr. McCallister, could it be that Ms. Sullivan has the Nokia in which we're interested?" Russo asked with a smirk. "We've no use for you either dead or in jail. So you could help us both out by playing for the FBI's team. By cooperating, you won't face obstruction of justice charges. How does that sound to you?"

Cocky sonofabitch, Ron thought as he licked blood on the inside of his swelling lip. He tried to not flex his jaw and to look calm before answering.

"The Nokia is the only bargaining chip that Carey and her son have now," he said. "I've grown quite attached to them. How do I know you'll have all of our backs if we do cooperate? Do you have anything else to show me beside your FBI identification, a sniper threat, and a rather rude slap to give me the notion that I can trust you?"

Ron watched as Russo took a step back and gave a grimace. He read some respect in it.

"Well, the slap and threats were to see how you'd react under pressure, whether you had principles or if you were a loose cannon," Russo said. "You really want to do good by Ms. Sullivan and her son, so you should work with us to put away those who threaten their lives. Help us wrap up our investigation and thwart these assholes and their rackets in Woolrich."

Ron thought it over. After a few minutes, he asked the three agents in the shack if they themselves had family.

"As I have one of the premier intelligence agencies in the United States at my disposal, I'd be very unlikely to face your situation, Mr. McCallister," Russo said. "But I'd like to give a fair shake to a man who wants to clear up the garbage in his town, I promise we'll put Ms. Sullivan and her son under protection. I only hope that my word will be enough."

Ron asked for a the pleasantness of a very rare cigarette. The sniper stuck a Lucky Strike in his mouth and lit it. Ron took a drag and allowed himself time to enjoy the savory, slightly painful sensation in his lungs. He blew the smoke toward the ceiling before nodding to his captors for another drag. After reaching the filter, he addressed the agents.

"Let me make a call that may help us all out. As far as Carey Sullivan and her son, you will not put them in any danger. If you keep a guard on them, then you will have my complete cooperation. Now give me my Samsung and a minute of privacy. If you want, one of you government-employed thugs can wait by the door and make sure an unarmed, slightly doped-up man doesn't pose a threat."

Russo uncuffed Ron, returned his cell phone, and motioned for the driver and the sniper to stand outside. He backed toward the door of the shack and took out his Glock .40 semiautomatic. Russo opened the door so that he was standing outside but could still keep an eye on his captive.

Ron called Carey and told her he was okay and working with the FBI. He told her not to worry, to get a good sleep back at the Travelodge, and to take care of her son.

"It'll be over soon enough if you just lie low and stay safe," Ron said. "I've made a deal with the devil, but it's the devil paid by our federal tax dollars. I need you to forward the numbers from

the Nokia to my cell phone, then return the
Nokia to the motel safe after you turn it off. Also
remember that I'll be damned if anyone gets in
the way of you, John, and I getting back
together."

Carey whispered an "I love you" before they
disconnected.

Russo came back into the shack and collected
the phone numbers and aliases that popped up
on Ron's Samsung some minutes later. He
nodded and showed Ron a bed to get some
sleep. He also set down a stainless steel flask
and handed him tomorrow's *Naperville Sun*
before leaving him for the night.

"There will be an FBI man checking in on you
periodically to ensure you're safe and still
cooperating," Russo told him. "I'll send two
agents to check-in occasionally on Ms. Sullivan
and her boy at the Travelodge. Tomorrow, you,
me, and my co-workers will attend the funeral of
my friend, Mike Simmons. You'll see that your
help in this case is already paying off if you read
the Sun I gave you. Get a good night's rest. Take
it easy tonight, Mr. McCallister; we're going to
need you tomorrow."

Ron poured himself a good two fingers of
what looked and smelled like Jack Daniels in the
cup sitting on the bed. He read the paper and
took interest in how his story would appear in
the local media the next morning.

"Former Strip Club Bouncer Exonerated," the
headline on the first page read. The rest of the
story, which proclaimed his and Carey's
innocence, made Ron want to cooperate. He
appreciated that Mike's FBI friend was putting an
iota of trust in him.

Ron read the rest of the paper and drank the

Jack. He was happy Russo had cut him off at half of what he wanted to drink. He was so relaxed that he wanted to keep on indulging. However, he knew he had to be sharp when watching Mike's funeral. He tried to not think of the next day as he tried to sleep. His thoughts wandered to those he loved before consciousness fled.

22

Graveyard

Nicky Ferranti took a hit of cocaine with his usual morning espresso as his attendant, driver, and most useful employee, Gino Drucci, whipped up some scrambled eggs and bacon. The boss read the funny pages in the Saturday *Naperville Sun*, basking in the light coming through the windows on the southeastern corner of his greystone house. He lit a Marlboro Light cigarette as he adjusted the robe that conformed to his bulky, 5-foot-10, frame.

A local escort he had ordered last night left around three hours earlier that morning. She had given him a massage earlier before trying to please him for about a half hour, to no avail. Before Ferranti could do something nasty with his frustration, she ducked out the back door of the house and to a nearby field. Fortunately for her, she had grabbed enough clothes to keep her very mild sense of modesty.

"Why aren't these stuck-up bitches better at getting a guy off? Isn't that what I pay them to do?" Ferranti asked Drucci while forking egg into his mouth.

Drucci didn't reply directly to the question because he had nothing polite to say. This was a smart thing. Instead, he only said: "I'm afraid that I'm not sure why less competent workers can't finish the job."

In the light of morning, Drucci had to be most patient. He gladly welcomed a change of subject.

"I think you'll agree with me that I ain't got to worry about any asshole police today if I pay my respects to the Simmons family," Ferranti said before he mashed down some bacon. "I am a small business owner whose 'investment in the community doesn't just end at dividends.' I'm thinking of running for mayor, or buying the office, after Peck reaches the end of his term. If you help me, how's about I put you in charge of communications?"

"Sounds wonderful," Drucci deadpanned. "For now, I'll help you pick out clothes. Do you want your black or dark blue suit for today's events? If you want my opinion, I'd go with the black with a light blue shirt. It's dressy, but still gives off a more friendly vibe."

Ferranti clasped his hands and puffed out his cheeks before praising the help.

"Lombardo told me I wouldn't be taking a chance with an educated man like you, Drucci. You can lay out the black and light blue. I'll be ready at noon. The funeral starts a half hour after, and I expect that will give me enough time to greet any saps for the media and pay my respects before watching Simmons get put in the ground. I really just want to get back to my club."

Before Ferranti had gotten ready and into the Lincoln, Drucci checked his Beretta 9 mm semiautomatic and put it in a shoulder holster before appearing in front of the passenger's side back seat. He then opened the door for Ferranti. Two goons, who were armed with Glock 18 automatics, followed in a Cadillac behind them.

It won't be long now, Drucci thought after he took his place in the driver's seat.

- - - - -

Carey Sullivan showed up at the edge of Clarendon Hills Cemetery in Woolrich just before the brief memorial started. In a black, knee-length pencil skirt and gray, button-down blouse, she wasn't dressed as formally as she would have liked to show her respects for Lizzy's husband. If she had decided to be completely cautious, she wouldn't be here.

But her heart told her to witness Mike's funeral rather than just wait in her motel room. Since she didn't have any other options, she had to bring John. Thankfully, he was more than happy to wait in the car and play with the stuffed bear Ron had given him earlier in the week.

Carey and John weren't yet aware that they were being watched.

She kept a discreet two hundred feet away from the gathering around her friend's grave. A large oak that hadn't yet sprouted leaves separated her from the callous, yet currently civil charades.

Nicky Ferranti and several other stocky, swarthy grunts were there. She recognized several of the faces as those who had held Lizzy hostage several days ago. Carey could almost hear the gritting of her own teeth as she restrained herself from lashing out. Seeing Mayor Rob Peck's smarmy face didn't help her disposition.

"Jesus Christ," Carey whispered to herself when she saw Ron emerging from a black Dodge Charger about five minutes after the political platitudes and prayers had started. "Surely he and the Feds aren't looking to start a shoot-out during a funeral."

By chance, Carey noticed someone with an FN Special Police Rifle in the bell tower of St. John's chapel, which adjoined the cemetery. The barrel seemed trained on Ferranti or someplace around him. She didn't even consider counteracting a public hit. She was concerned about any danger to Ron, but even more so about drawing attention to her and John.

She watched with worry from a distance as Ferranti dropped a split second after a loud crack pierced the air. The sniper's .308 round ripped through Ferranti's temple before chaos erupted.

Mayor Peck quickly ducked for cover as the shot went off. His security surrounded him and escorted him to safety within five seconds.

The attending DuPage County Sheriff joined several deputies in attempting to contain the ensuing panic. Two deputies stormed the chapel, following the sound of the shot. The assassin shot one of the pursuing deputies in the shoulder before the other deputy shot him in the chest.

The funeral party had abruptly dispersed in all directions, save for the surely dead Ferranti and one of his loyal men. All the rest of the mob men, including the one who drove Ferranti to the graveyard and others who had held Lizzy hostage, didn't hesitate to get back in their luxury sedans to escape.

Having come within fifty feet of the service, Ron ran back to the where he had arrived. He got in the Charger in while two men in black suits got out and ran toward Ferranti and the remaining loyal man. The man shot at the two Feds only to be put down with a bullet to the brain.

Within a few minutes, DuPage County Sheriff's personnel secured the area around the chapel and the burial site. The Sheriff tended to his wounded deputy as a lone EMT and a late-arriving squad car from the Woolrich Police Department showed themselves.

Despite the mob hits, law enforcement chaos, and the sight of Ron going with a couple of men in black suits to track down mobsters, Carey was most startled when she felt a gentle prodding to her behind. She spun around and saw John with a worried look on his face that echoed her sentiments on the whole situation.

Before he could start crying, Carey lifted him up and tried to casually make her way back to the Jeep, parked just over one hundred feet away. She didn't notice anyone from the Sheriff's office paying them attention. She chalked it up to the distance between them and more pressing events surrounding the dead Ferranti.

Carey got in the Jeep after putting John in the back seat and buckling him in. On the way back to the Travelodge, she called Ron's Samsung after putting her Motorola Razr on speakerphone. She was worried when he didn't answer but tried not to show it because John was looking to her for a sense of calm. She hummed with the radio as she gave a smile to him in the rearview mirror.

She had a harder time maintaining her cool after the mirror showed that she wasn't alone. A black Ford Expedition was trailing her. She decided to pull into a Denny's that she saw and get a bite to eat and try to get a view of her tail. John loved Denny's and he usually charmed the waitstaff for freebies.

Win-win, she thought. *John will be thrilled to act like a kid again and we'll get a bite. If I find out more about the Expedition, we can maybe make it to our room at the Travelodge with some sense of peace.*

After she parked in the Denny's parking lot, she stuffed her Glock in her purse before taking John by the hand and leading him inside. They took a booth away from the entrance and windows. She kept her eyes locked on the door for suspicious-looking hit men or government cleaners.

Well aren't you a sweetie?" a trim, middle-aged waitress with the name tag that read Delores said to John. "You get complimentary fries if you want a steak."

"I saw a dead man," John replied before Carey pinched his cheeks and pecked him on the forehead.

"Today was his first funeral. It was a friend of the family, and even at three, he can tell something's off," Carey said, giving a friendly, but forced smile. "He'll be better when he gets something in his tummy. Could we get a strawberry shake with two straws as we peruse the menu for a minute? Thanks a lot, hon."

Delores returned a tight but polite grin and nodded before she made her way back to her station.

- - - - -

Agent Matt Russo drove the Charger within one hundred feet of a Cadillac in the tail of the mob motorcade. His new, somewhat coerced help, Ron McCallister, rode in the back while his partner, the sniper from the previous evening, rode shotgun. His partner spoke on his Blackberry with desk jockeys at Chicago Headquarters.

From what Russo could hear, "home office" was agitated about Ferranti's death and the attention gained from the DuPage County Sheriff's department. He thought he heard "Goddamned press!" several times. He was glad that he had chosen the less stressful task of following behind the mob at over eighty miles per hour.

"When will we make arrests, Matt?" his partner asked him. "'Home office' wants to know if it will be worth the effort. They don't want us to put FBI authorities in the limelight unless we can make it count."

Agent Russo grew hot under the collar but didn't want to take it out on his partner as the latter finished whatever he was talking about. Federal waste and bureaucracy were the real focus of his frustration.

"Please tell those pencil-pushing pricks, I mean, 'higher-ups,' that we are acting on field intelligence that should bring down organized crime not only in Woolrich, but also lead to information on associates of Joey Lombardo," he said. "We can't guarantee arrests tonight, but when they are made, they will count big time."

After his partner relayed the information to "home office" in Chicago, Russo fist bumped him before a .308 round went through the windshield on the passenger's side. Russo decelerated as quickly as he could and calmly pulled over to the side of the road. The Charger behind him was less adaptive after a second .308 shot busted through its windshield. The sudden swerves ended in a six car pileup and several explosions.

"Damn it!" Agent Russo shouted before he started a more indirect route to Starlet's Alley. He swerved to offset any potential shots from an enemy sniper. He threw his dead partner's phone out of the window and didn't answer his own cell phone for the rest of the drive. He returned Ron's Glock and handed him an extra clip.

"You might need this this, buddy," Russo said. "You're hereby unofficially assisting the FBI Organized Crime Program. Congratulations. We can have a ceremony later."

"I can help you put some real sociopaths behind bars if those at 'home office' let us," Ron replied. "If we live through this, you are buying a round of whiskeys; I'll pick up the tip."

"It would be my first drink in six years and then some... Let's just get the bad guys first."

Agent Russo and Ron arrived at Starlet's Alley well after the mob had returned. Russo closed his dead partner's eyes and hoped to give him a proper burial. For now, he and his new assistant had to confront events on the ground.

- - - - -

Half an hour before Ron and Agent Russo arrived at Starlet's Alley, Gino Drucci ordered three goons to put all the cocaine and paraphernalia in a Chevy van and drive toward the hideout in nearby Lisle. Following the van was a Cadillac carrying a bound, gagged, and heavily drugged Lizzy Simmons.

In his own mind, Drucci was more equipped than Ferranti to handle the mob's business in Woolrich and Chicago's other western suburbs. After he gave the order to stash the evidence, he changed into a pinstripe Armani suit and ordered a Perrier instead of a Glenlivet. He sat at a discreet booth as he got down to the task of hiring a new girl since recent decreases in staff. His predecessor had started the search, but Drucci found the task less of a distraction.

The presumed mob leader admired his paramour's firm behind as the college-aged boy brought him his water and returned a wink before salaciously sauntering back to the bar. The breasts, hips, and legs on stage didn't pique his interest other than their ability to bring in legitimate money and cover for cocaine commerce.

Finally, the one who deserves to be in charge has found his place, Drucci thought. *The seller should never be a user of his own products, sexual or medicinal. Such habits can get too expensive. Bravo to my fickle friends in the Feds who efficiently finish off Ferranti.*

Drucci's first applicant for the stage was a strawberry blonde about the age of his boy toy. His interest in her naturally tan complexion, healthy bust, small waist, and the bulge of her behind was strictly professional. He gestured for her to her sit across from him. He immediately decided not to hire her when she stiffly sat down without any attempt to flash her assets. She didn't even take off her conservative glasses and seemed too nervous to smile.

She's got the goods, but not what passes as talent to make brutish breeders throw the big bucks on stage, he thought. *Might as well get through the boilerplate questions while I move on to the next one.*

After he told the current applicant that she should wait for his call, Drucci found greater prospects in a dark-haired Latina that followed. The latter wore such a loose silk blouse that her nearly cantaloupe-sized breasts nearly spilled out when she bent in his direction while sitting. He hired her after listening to her accent during introductions. He was happy to return to mob matters that didn't involve the intricacies of women.

He gestured for his paramour to join him at his booth after telling the new Latina hire to fetch him a club soda and lime from the bar. She returned with the drink before a bouncer took her to have a look at the clothes she'd be shedding on stage.

As happy hour approached, Drucci fingered the Beretta 9 mm semiautomatic that lay beside him as he sipped his soda. He admired his foresight to arm his bouncers and guards with Glock 18 automatics. He gave a sultry wink to his paramour, Joe Nowak, who sipped a Cosmopolitan between lightly glossed lips.

"Joe, tell me what guys see in that thing dancing on stage," he said. "She has globs of silicone bouncing on top of what would be a fine set of pectoral muscles. I'd rather have a cock-fighting ring if it was legal and made as much money. A nice set of strapping young boys could also set up the ring for the cocks. Now that's a show I'd like to see."

Nowak laughed as he took a gulp of his drink.

"I think these breeders think of their moms and sucking on the teat when ogling these skanks," Nowak said. "I was a psychology major for a semester at college before I started dealing. I totally agree with Sigmund Freud. You should have seen what a sorority chick would do to one of my frat boy friends for a little bit of candy."

Remember, you didn't start dating this kid because of his class, Drucci thought. He ordered a waiter to bring another Cosmo for his company and an Old Rip Van Winkle French Manhattan for himself. *If I am to be a major player for mob interests in the western burbs, I might as well drink like it.*

"If you stay away from the Feds and cops who may visit later on tonight, I assure you that you'll get more than your fair share of candy." Drucci said. "Not only that, but you'll be a cabana boy for a leader in the mob. I can get you all the coke, all the money, all the prestige you need.

The sky's the limit."

"I'll do whatever you want, Gino," he said. "If you need me to smooth things over with the authorities, I'm your man. I'm a real charmer."

"I know what your talents are, Joe," Drucci said, betraying no laughter that undermined his position. His immediate worry was Kendra De Silva, whom he considered an underage time bomb. Aside from Lombardo's consent and the objectionable way Ferranti conducted business, he killed the Sicilian because of the chances he had taken with volatile actors.

Drucci decided to keep Kendra in the trailer behind Starlet's Alley as he figured out more plans for her. He tried to relax for the evening and act the part of the right-hand man who was dealing with business after the death of a mentor. It was harder than he had originally thought. He hated the Sicilian and was happy a sniper had silenced him.

23

Competence and Lack Thereof

Two FBI agents tasked with keeping Carey Sullivan safe got out of their Ford Expedition. They suspected that she saw them following her, so they tried to be less aggressive when they approached her as she came out of the Denny's alone. They made a huge mistake in not looking out for their own safety at first. They didn't even get a chance to identify themselves.

Carey swiftly cold-cocked one of the FBI agents unconscious after luring him for a light for a rare cigarette. She was ten feet outside of the Denny's, where she had left John to charm Delores. As the one quickly fell to the ground, the other made her consider that she had made a rash decision.

The other man pulled his sidearm on her, showed his FBI badge, and told her to put her hands behind her head as he professionally frisked her. He had been tasked to protect her, which meant that he had to make sure that she didn't give him a beating first. The handcuffs he assertively put on her gave him a sense of peace.

Carey was thankful that the agent did not lewdly lurk during his search. Then again, it was better for him to make her feel less threatened than she already did.

After he relieved her of her Glock, removed the clip, and engaged the safety, he led her back into "America's Diner." He took her with a firm, but not too rough, grip on her left bicep toward John and Delores at the back table. The agent showed his badge before he laid down enough money to pay for the shake.

"Hon, can I have that shake to go?" Carey asked Delores. "This guy might be taking me into custody or whatever, but I sure as hell am not going to deny my son a childhood treat while that happens."

She then told Delores to take $10 out of the wallet in her purse as tip. The FBI agent nodded consent before he took John's hand.

The waitress gingerly searched for the tip and returned the purse to John. Delores forced a world-weary grin.

"I'll bring the shake outside in a minute if you take your son and follow your escort out of here," she said. "I promise. We just don't want any trouble inside the restaurant. I'll see you out front in a bit."

After the three exited and went to the Ford Expedition, the FBI agent locked Carey and her son in the back seat for everyone's protection. He walked back toward his prostrate partner. He tried to revive him and waited to collect the shake with a confidence that was soon to be deflated.

- - - - -

FBI Agent Matt Russo focused binoculars on the two guards in front of Starlet's Alley and tried to make the semblance of a plan for him and Ron. They were hiding in brush about one hundred yards or so from the strip club. Russo was not expecting any sort of backup to arrive.

"Chicago headquarters is hardly concerned with the burbs," he explained to Ron. "Even though this is where most of the mob's business is moving, it isn't sexy to chase after hoodlums in Woolrich. I hope it doesn't come as a shock that the federal government would employ some who don't make the public interest a first priority."

Ron appreciated Russo's jab to unearned authority.

"I'll help because I agree that these assholes should get served some justice," he said. "Hell, I'll give it all I got, backup be damned. I've been in shadier situations, only then it was with more firepower."

Russo gave his first genuine smile since meeting Ron under less-than-cordial conditions.

"I need you to go check out that trailer behind Starlet's Alley," he said. "These mob assholes might be keeping a trump card in there. I'll take out the hired help and draw attention to the front of the operation."

"Yes siree," Ron said with sarcasm he reserved for those giving orders who weren't paying him. "I just hope government lawyers will know what to do with the hundreds of dollars in my frozen savings account if luck isn't on my side."

Russo shook his head as he pulled out a Heckler & Koch MP5 from the trunk of the Charger and wished Ron good luck.

"Your assistance and my fine piece of machinery here will be all I need for the near future," he said. "With what these jokers have said on tapped phones, the notes Mike messaged me, and your future testimony, these mobsters should be found guilty beyond a doubt to any jury. We're just here to grab the glory. Back in the Army, my CO ordered me to deal with a lot of shit bags myself. The most competent soldiers get the hardest jobs. Hooah, brother!"

Ron just nodded his head and chuckled lightly before he crept in the brush toward the trailer.

He heard gun fire back and forth before the guards out front wailed in pain when Russo shot them in the kneecaps. Ron smiled when the two guards smoking cigarettes outside the trailer ran toward the entrance of the strip club. He wished he could've seen the expressions on their faces when they found their fellow thugs writhing in pain.

- - - - -

Ron easily sneaked to the entrance of the trailer when the hired muscle had left. The trailer looked serene, empty, and almost peaceful. Ron sized it up the situation before making a move to open the unlocked metal front door.

"Jesus Christ!" Ron yelled as a sharp steak knife hit the wall nearly five inches above and to the left of his head. "I'm here to help, you dolt!"

A familiar looking, underage girl in a leopard-print bra and skintight, black, vinyl pants tossed a paring knife that stuck in his left shoulder. He was able to squeeze off a shot from his Glock to her offending right hand. He didn't care who heard the commotion as long as the shot disabled the knife-throwing maniac.

Unfortunately for Ron, that's not what happened.

The clearly doped-up teenager lunged at Ron before he could aim and fire another non-lethal, disabling shot. She acted like she didn't even feel her wounded hand as she rammed into his body. The momentum and surprise knocked him to the ground outside of the trailer. Her knees on either side of his rib cage, she lifted a baseball-sized rock above her emaciated left shoulder. He made the connection to her identity.

She's a little different in the flesh, Ron thought quickly. *Mayor De Silva's coked-up daughter is looking ragged.*

"Kendra, what the hell are you doing?" he yelled before easily knocking the rock away with with a smack with his right hand. His mind worked quickly as pain shot from his left shoulder to the incisors in his mouth. "You gotta calm down, kid, or we're gonna end up in a graveyard like your father."

Kendra hesitated as her leopard print clad chest began to take in larger breaths. Ron could feel her legs loosen and see her face become somewhat relaxed before she rolled off of him. She immediately curled into a fetal position and started sobbing.

"Mom's dead too," she said out loud for the first time. "I don't care if Dad's dead, but why'd Mom have to die?"

"I don't want to have to hurt you," Ron said. "but if we don't get the hell out of here, we're all screwed."

That's when the crazy hit Kendra again.

"Why the hell should I trust a guy who shot me?" she asked as they both shakily tried to stand up.

Ron deflected her left hand before she could pull the knife out of his shoulder. Instead of a verbal response, he smacked her in the gut to send her back to the ground. He was actually somehow relieved when he heard police sirens, likely responding to reports of automatic weapons fire.

One of Woolrich's finest dosed Ron with volts from a taser gun after showing up. As he fell to the ground, he felt some satisfaction that Kendra received a reflection of the same volts by having grabbed his ankle. They were both incapacitated.

The responding officers administered first-aid

to Ron and Kendra before they were put in ambulances to Woolrich Memorial Hospital. As morphine was shot into Ron's vein, he felt a pleasant chill before his senses dulled. The entire world became an oddly reassuring dream.

Aunt Peggy, Carey, John, Ervin, Lizzy, Brian, and I will all live out in the countryside, hunting for food and living off the land, Ron thought, growing loopy before unconsciousness overtook him.

- - - - -

Delores drove her rusty 1995 Oldsmobile to her apartment in Lisle. Carey followed with the Jeep Wrangler as John slept while buckled in the back seat. After the women had parked, Carey cradled John in her arms before she joined Delores to sit on the warm hood of the Oldsmobile. The latter lit a Lucky Strike cigarette.

Carey declined the offer of another smoke before she slung her son's sleepy body against her bosom. She was more than happy to simply breath in the cool spring air and watch the stars in the clear night sky.

"Thank you for helping me and letting me give you a few bucks for a night on your futon," Carey said. "There's only one man that I trust in this world, and he's off to heaven-knows-where with some Feds. If you get any harassment from the cops, I'll deny you helped me."

Back in the Denny's parking lot, Delores had distracted the FBI man by "accidentally" dropping John's shake after she came outside with the to-go order. She seized the opportunity to knock the Fed to the ground with a kick and secure his hands behind his back with the strings of her apron. She had to get Carey out of the Ford Expedition to help drag the subdued, barely conscious agents back to the to SUV.

Carey took the Ford and the two agents to a back road. Once there, she cuffed the agents; wrists together through the steering wheel before they could fully wake up. Delores was quick to pick up Carey and John and return them to their vehicle. Carey took the keys from the Expedition and tossed them somewhere in a roadside ditch.

As they currently relaxed under the night sky, Delores said she didn't regret any of it, or offering Carey a place to stay for the night. Her shift was nearly done anyway, so there was no money to be lost. She figured that anyone who would trust her kid to her and give a 200% tip wouldn't mind a little gratuity in return. She flicked her cigarette before reassuring Carey that she had broken the law for similar reasons.

"I don't like the damned police," Delores said. "Your boy is cute and you love him. I tried to take my daughter from an abusive husband after knocking him out. I got arrested and neither of them will speak to me anymore. Mother to mother, I'm all about helping a woman who loves her kid. It helps that you're a good tipper."

Delores received something that she least expected out of another human being when Carey hugged her while still holding her son. An understanding between the three of them formed in the instant before they trudged up the stairs of the apartment building.

Carey made John comfortable on the futon. She then happily joined a kindred soul for a needed nightcap.

Delores pulled out a pint of Jim Beam and poured them each two fingers as they stood in the kitchenette. They spoke about their mistakes with men, those who could be trusted and how they planned to make their situations better.

Little did Carey know that Lizzy was holed up with mobsters a few miles away. If she had known, she would've let John sleep, drove the Jeep to the hideout, and called Ron to meet her there. But she didn't know and worried when she still couldn't reach the last man she trusted. Delores went to her bedroom to sleep at quarter to midnight after another hug.

Soon after that, Carey got some water for her son and cuddled with him. She joined him in sleep on the futon soon after.

She slept until nine the next morning. Delores gently woke them and allowed them to partake in generic Cheerios, skim milk, instant coffee, and juice for John. The day was going to get busy.

24

Thunder Before the Storm

Ron woke up Sunday morning to see the familiar, beige walls of Woolrich Memorial hospital. It wasn't any more pleasant than he remembered from the last time, and he expected efforts by so-called law enforcement to make him even less comfortable. There was nothing to do but wait for someone to kill him, interrogate him, or maybe both.

There was a knock at the door, and he realized he couldn't get up because his arms were handcuffed to the bed. The fuzz learned from the last time that restraints made from anything other than stainless steel wasn't enough to hold him. He watched as a man with an off-the-rack suit addressed him in a deeper voice than expected, given the receding brown, silver-streaked hairline and dry, thin lips.

"Mr. McCallister, my name is Dave Holbert. I'm Chicago's FBI Special Agent in Charge," the man in the monkey suit said. "Why don't you start with your side of the story. I'd also appreciate if you told me what Agent Matt Russo promised you?"

Well, hello Agent Dave, Ron thought. *I'm wondering what more qualified dipshits have to say.*

Since Ron felt trapped and helpless in the face of the handcuffs and a boring bureaucrat, so his more diplomatic and calculating side won out. He told parts of the truth in hopes of learning something more substantive in return.

Ron explained that after being framed for murder, he had been killing or injuring gunmen to defend the lives of himself and his friend, Carey, who had been a co-worker at Starlet's Alley. He also wanted to help out Carey's young son, John.

After Ron had witnessed the deaths of his acquaintance, Mike Simmons, and numerous bad guys, Agent Russo contacted him. Ron felt that any past suspicion of his alleged criminal activity was wiped out by articles in the Saturday *Naperville Sun*. He and Russo agreed to work together to make some things right. They teamed-up to confront the gangsters and politicians responsible for the latest spate of violence in the city of Woolrich.

He sighed after his explanation and smiled at his Latina nurse, who had curves like Carey, but with caramel-toned instead of alabaster skin. His thoughts drifted to Carey and her son before the pencil-pusher interrupted him.

"Our man, Russo, may have gone too far by shooting bouncers at Starlet's Alley," Holbert said, adjusting his collar in what Ron read as nervousness. "When police responded to the gunfire, they didn't find any drugs or other illegal paraphernalia inside the club. The only thing out of the ordinary that they found were four bouncers with holes in their kneecaps and a few drunks bent on disturbing the peace. No sign of our agent. You happen to know where our man Russo is? Any cooperation on your part is greatly appreciated."

He's probably doing your job and trying to find the criminals implied by phone taps and the murders meant to cover up the mob's drug operation, Ron thought. *Wouldn't the taps key you into Russo's investigation? This dickhead is too shady to be on the up and up.*

"Can't say I've any clue on the whereabouts of Agent Russo," Ron said after an awkward silence. "I would expect him to be following up on any leads to aid his investigation. I'm not sure I trust him, but I respect his tenacity and grit. By the way, am I under arrest? Are there charges being brought up on me? Your man ruled me an innocent. What gives?"

The suit opposite Ron adopted a look of false concern by blowing air to puff out the round, rosy cheeks on either side of his chin.

"It's all part of the process, Mr. McCallister," Holbert said. "The FBI doesn't cross jurisdictional lines when it comes to local misdemeanors. You'll have to ask the Woolrich police. However, you should know that if the local force mistreats you, the FBI will start a full investigation with internal affairs into whether it has been handled adequately. We follow complaints about local law enforcement with great diligence."

Asshole, Ron thought after Holbert nodded and left the room. He asked for water from the nurse and noticed the catheter connected to his urethra. *Damn it, it's gonna be quite a bit more difficult if I try to escape this time.*

His angst-filled thoughts didn't last long as he received another nice dose of morphine. The Latina nurse gave the shot, bending over his head to reveal cleavage barely hidden by her teasingly-unbuttoned neckline.

She wished him *buenos noches* before she refastened a few buttons and left the room. Ron would've frowned, had he been able to, when two men in operating masks and scrubs wheeled him from the room and toward an ambulance. As the siren began to wail, he fell into another sleep as chills raced through his veins.

His dreams weren't so pleasant this time around.

- - - - -

Gino Drucci had a shot of Tullamore Dew Irish whiskey just after the clock read noon. He didn't usually drink before five p.m., but the previous twenty-four hours helped him actually grasp some respect for the horny drug addicts who preceded him. Joey Lombardo had called his iPhone just two hours into the morning to name him as *numero uno* for the mob in Woolrich, and the realization made him nervous.

How could any anyone play it cool with so many sexual and sedative influences around him? he thought. He sipped his whiskey and lit a cigarette inside Starlet's Alley in defiance of the law. *Only after I inherited the joint did some nut job decide to exchange automatic weapons fire with my guards.*

The night before, Drucci didn't bother looking after his paramour, Joe Nowak. He allowed his inebriated lover to punch a fine member of the local police. Heavily-lined pockets and Drucci's playing dumb likely kept circumstances copacetic. Nowak became collateral damage through his own stupidity.

That's the price others must pay for me to stay in charge, he thought. *I gotta pay too, and the local rent-a-cops seemed to enjoy my adequate-enough acting. The hardest part was keeping a straight face.*

"Surely, you didn't find any illegal drugs or paraphernalia on anyone from my predecessor's employ," Drucci had said. "As acting manager, I'm more inclined to run a tight ship than to waste time breaking the law."

The police then assured Drucci that they

hadn't found anything and that his staff had complied fully once the parking lot gunman stopped shooting.

Drucci realized the biggest threat to his management of Saturday's events was that police had not yet found whoever was shooting at the club. There were already tough guys taking care of Kendra, Lizzy, and the good Samaritan who broke into the trailer.

He tried to think of other ways his takeover of Woolrich's cocaine distribution was threatened as he finished his Sunday lunchtime whiskey. He thought of the former stripper, Carey Sullivan, and realized that she might be his other volatile, less tracked loose end.

Good thing I've made allegiances with like-minded guys in the FBI, Drucci thought. *I should eventually head over to Lisle to see how my guys are dealing with more immediately-pressing variables and potential bargaining chips.*

- - - - -

Lizzy Simmons struggled against the ropes that bound her wrists behind her back in the basement where she was held. She discovered that she was in Lisle by listening to the banter of those who guarded her. She also figured that she was in a basement because of the darkness that surrounded her except when a guard opened the door up a stairway. Someone came occasionally to give her some water or let her relieve herself in a bucket that she could smell across the room. The cold cement floor also helped wake her.

Withdrawal's a bitch, she thought. *There's gotta be a way out. I may have to put up a fight. Goddammit, my nose is running and I can't scratch.*

A light turned on above her left shoulder as she heard the guards lugging a heavy package down the stairs.

"That queer, Drucci, told us this guy's one of the only jerks who's out to get us," a guard said. "Our gal in the ward got his name as Ron McCallister. He'll wake up in pain from lack of morphine in a few hours. Drucci says he'll be here soon enough to ask him about his friend with the automatic and anything else."

Lizzy got a look at Ron. Even in the dim light, he looked familiar. She hoped that she could rouse him for help between the arrival of more guards or whoever was in charge. Drucci was one of the other familiar names she heard. She hoped to find out more about the truth before her new roommate could be interrogated. The other guard kept on blabbing like the useful idiot that he was.

"After Ferranti got knocked off, Drucci gave us Kendra frickin' De Silva to look after as well," he said. "I really don't like the heat from that, but I don't think she'll be much of a problem. She's too warped on coke to notice anything."

The guards closed the doors as Lizzy remembered why the name Kendra was important. She knew that ultimate salvation would come from getting the lump of Ron's body awake. Lizzy wriggled herself over to his unconscious, prostrate, but only handcuffed body. She began to kick him in what she assumed were his buttocks. She didn't want to hurt anything on him that might be useful. Still, her kicks reflected the fervor with which she wanted him to rejoin the conscious world.

I shouldn't hurt him, she thought. *He might be my opening to find out more. He at least might be be able to help me scratch my nose*.

- - - - -

Carey was thankful for Delores and her hospitality. She held John's sleepy body in her arms as the three went down the stairs from the apartment to their cars.

Once in the Jeep, Carey noticed a Lincoln driving down the street. She figured such a car was a rarity in Delores' part of town and felt an informed compulsion to follow it safely from a distance. She remembered seeing quite a few similar cars yesterday afternoon at Clarendon Hills Cemetery. She quickly exited the Jeep and ran to Delores' Oldsmobile.

"I'm gonna go find out if the jerks in that Lincoln can lead me to my friend or give me any information," Carey said to her. "The last time I saw them was the last time I saw my friend, Ron. There's bound to be some sort of connection. If you've got to get to work, I understand. But I'd like to keep my boy at a safe distance."

Delores returned a grim look and shrugged in her Denny's uniform.

"I'll take John back to my place," Delores said. "I've got a neighbor who I trust to watch over him. It'd be better than bringing him to Denny's. I've got enough of my own problems. I can't take off of work to watch your son, no matter how cute he is."

Carey nodded her assent before she got her son from the Jeep so he could take Delores' hand back to her apartment. The women gave brief hugs before they did what needed to be done.

Carey sped the Jeep along the road and slowed when she encountered the Lincoln. She tried to be subtle as she followed and parked over one hundred yards down the street from where the other car stopped. When she got out, she saw the a red-brick, one-story house that looked peaceful enough from the outside.

She stalked toward the house, clutching her Glock in her right hand. She breathed in forcefully as she recognized one of the ruffians who had been with Nicky Ferranti at Mike Simmons' memorial.

Carey switched off the safety and made sure there was a round in the chamber. She wouldn't hesitate pulling the trigger to put a stop to the bastards threatening those she loved. She pushed aside any worries so that she could focus.

25

The Main Event

Agent Matt Russo kept surveillance with his binoculars about one hundred yards away from the Lisle red brick hideout in a field next door. He recognized Carey Sullivan and watched as she crept up to the driveway that led toward the front door. He took in the strong calf muscles bustling under Carey's almost dressy black skirt before he checked his libido. He noticed the handgun in her right hand and surveyed the surroundings for possible threats.

Damn, that lady shows more cojones *than many of my fellow field agents*, he thought, smiling. *I'd recommend her for the FBI in a heartbeat if she and I live through this.*

Russo watched as Carey nearly knocked out an inattentive man in the driveway and yelled to two additional thugs in front of the house to put their guns down. She ducked behind the Lincoln when they shot at her. She returned fire and hit them each below the waist. She took the one she had punched as her guide and hostage. The two geniuses she shot writhed in pain on the front porch before she sent them to dreamland with kicks to the head. She slowly entered the hideout through the front door, her hostage in front of her.

Russo was about to run toward the hideout and when he saw Gino Drucci being driven up in another Lincoln. The current mob boss exited his vehicle with three other guys. They all carried Glock 18 automatics with 33-round magazines as they stalked toward the Lisle hideout. The two thugs bleeding out front clearly put them on edge

Russo had to draw any fire away from Carey's actions. He knew he needed firepower to be effective at this point. He knelt on the ground after he took his H&K MP5 and put a bead on Drucci's calf muscle. After he positioned himself, he took a deep breath and quietly exhaled before slowly pulling the trigger.

As Drucci fell and screamed in pain, his men aimed toward the field and fired their Glocks. Russo, meanwhile, trained his sub machine gun at a level of the kneecaps of Drucci's men. Two of them became in need of a trip to the emergency room before the third got off a lucky shot to the FBI agent's right shoulder.

The third man in Drucci's group checked in briefly with his boss before being loudly ordered by a wounded Drucci to "find out what the hell is going on in the house."

Russo gritted his teeth and swore under his breath. Thoughts of helping Carey drove him to put his pain aside. He hustled as quickly as he could toward the injured mobsters outside.

These sons of bitches aren't out of commission yet, he thought.

- - - - -

Carey could hear the staccato blasts of automatic weapons while her hostage unwillingly tied up a goon who had been guarding Kendra in the back of the house. The goon nodded toward the basement when Kendra served him several slaps. Carey quickly headed downstairs with her hostage just as gunshots outside died down.

The hostage led her to Lizzy and Ron. She was surprised at seeing her two good friends in the basement. Carey knocked her hostage unconscious with a blow to the temple before trying to understand any more complexities to the matter. The scene before her didn't make much sense to someone who wasn't suffering from drug-withdrawal nor a kick to the head.

Lizzy stopped kicking the bound Ron after Carey whistled and stomped her foot to get some attention. Lizzy smiled and called to Carey, her voice raspy with excited, erratic explanation.

"I was trying to help him rescue us, so I decided to kick him," Lizzy said. She scratched her head with the floor as if she had spiders crawling on her.

Carey stifled a nervous laugh before taking charge of the situation.

She shushed Lizzy before untying her and a scuffed-up Ron. Like a parent to a child, she explained to Lizzy that she shouldn't have kicked the barely conscious man because he was a friend. Carey rightfully decided not to give either of her friends anything that could be used as a weapon. She told them they had to make a fast exit to safety and that Lizzy would have to help her support Ron so they could make their way up the stairwell.

At the top of the stairs, Carey peeked through a crack between the door and the frame. When she surveyed the situation, she saw a thug who had likely come from the gunfire outside. He had Kendra by the hair and was threatening her with his Glock 18 while she cried hysterically.

Carey aimed her gun before the thug advanced and aimed toward the door where she was taking cover. She quickly prayed that her bullet would take out the aggressor as Lizzy worked to support Ron on one of the stairs just below the top. She squeezed the trigger twice after letting out a quiet breath. A cadenced eruption of bullets fired at the door and ceiling of the house. Carey's eyes closed.

- - - - -

Gino Drucci crawled to the house using his forearms and uninjured leg. Pain shot through his injured calf muscle as he heard two quick gun blasts before about a dozen pops from an automatic punctured the air. The sounds of a wailing woman and of things crashing inside the house piqued his curiosity.

Kendra came out the front door. She was panting in a haze of drug-withdrawal before Drucci got off a shot that took out her left leg. After falling to a prostrate position on the front porch, she took off the shoe on her right foot before throwing it at him.

Drucci started crawling up the steps of the house. Before he could get a second, lethal shot at Kendra, a .40 caliber round ripped through his shooting arm. Agent Russo soon came out of the nearby field.

Russo pacified Drucci with a kick to his temple. He pointed the Glock .40 semiautomatic at the mobster with his uninjured left arm while making sure his target was unconscious. He went in the house after confirming Kendra was more or less safe and that the four hostiles outside were incapacitated. He didn't expect what he saw inside, which was saying a lot for a jaded FBI agent looking for organized crime in Chicago's suburbs. To his contentment, he'd seen and expected much worse.

He telephoned for backup from the Downtown Chicago FBI office and requested the DuPage County Sheriff's office be called to help clean up the mess.

I think I've earned those steaks and a night

Hangover, Part II

Ron McCallister woke up about five days after the Lisle shootout alone, peering through crusty eyelids at the all-too-familiar beige walls of Woolrich Memorial Hospital. He was happy to not be restrained by handcuffs or leather straps, but was still damned thirsty despite an intravenous stream of nutrients and drugs. He buzzed the pager near his left hand to find out any news from the outside world and get something to drink. He wanted a Miller-Beam boiler maker, but he didn't dare push his luck. There were no signs that he was under arrest yet.

A nun dressed in a traditional habit entered his room. Her face, without a trace of makeup, was nurturing and kind. It instantly put him at ease. She put a gentle, dry hand on his head before they had a chance to talk. He noticed the sun's rays on the wall showing that it might be either early evening or midmorning.

"Hello, ma'am, if it's at all possible, could I get a water or juice?" he asked with a voice that was more gravelly than usual. "I'm parched and would really appreciate it."

The nun introduced herself and answered.

"My name's Sister Maria Deluca," she said. "I'll page the nurse for water. The doctor is done with any procedures that would otherwise prohibit taking fluids. A man with the FBI wants to ask you a few questions when you feel fit for it. Until then, I may be able to help with matters of the soul or the mind."

Ron returned the cordial smile that was given to him. They waited several minutes before a nurse brought an insulated hospital mug of water and positioned a straw to his mouth. He swallowed several gulps after the nurse left.

"Could you tell me what's happened to my friend, Carey Sullivan?" he asked with slightly smoother speech.

"I'm afraid that she was seriously injured," Sister Maria said. "We should pray for her. Doctors have been doing their best for the past week. They are optimistic that she will recover in the coming days. The hand of God can only help."

"I'm not a religious man, sister. But if you think praying will help, I'm inclined to agree with you. Would you kindly lead?"

Sister Maria gracefully reached out to Ron as he awkwardly took her hands.

"Repeat after me," she said. "Hail Mary, full of grace..."

Ron repeated the words of the prayer. He hoped that the attention of doctors and whatever cosmic grace was out there would be able to help Carey. He hadn't expected a flesh-baring gal to grab his heart so firmly, but what he really admired was her spirit and her passion towards those to whom she was loyal. She could react rationally while still maintaining a warm strength.

"Amen," they said together, before enjoying a few minutes of oddly pleasant silence.

"Can you tell me about my other friends, Lizzy Simmons and Carey's son, John?" he asked her.

Sister Maria took some time before responding.

"Lizzy is terribly distraught, physically from the drugs and emotionally and spiritually from the loss of her husband," she said. "However, reuniting with her son, Brian, lifted her spirits enough for her to be discharged after the doctor gave permission.

"I saw her in the chapel today, and she is checking in on Carey. John is scared but fortunately too young to worry like an adult. A worker with DuPage County Child Support Services is keeping an eye on him until we know more about his mom. I keep an eye on them and hope that God shows me a way to help them."

Ron thanked Sister Maria for the updates and prayers. He said that he would not mind talking to John, unless she advised against it. He figured the boy might need more time.

"I think it would be best to let John cope with the new situation and surroundings before seeing you," she said. "I sense that you care for him, so I pray you can muster some patience. Since you are not a family member or legal guardian, I doubt regulations would let you see him regardless of what I think."

"Patience has always been something I've struggled with, Sister," he said. "I'll do my best and defer to your advice."

Sister Maria spent another fifteen minutes with Ron chatting with him about life, his background, and his dear Aunt Peggy before she excused herself to visit with other patients. He told her that she could let the FBI man talk to him whenever. They exchanged a warm smile when she stood by the door to his room.

"You're a good person, and I wish the best for you and your service, Sister," he said. "Hope to see you around. Take good care and know that you're making a difference."

She thanked him and blessed him in return

before going out the door.

Ron knew his next visitor would be less gentle and charming. Still, he figured the dialogue would be useful in putting an end to events of the past few weeks.

- - - - -

Special Agent Dave Holbert didn't knock before entering Ron's room a while later. Holbert still seemed to Ron more of an uptight bean-counter than an investigator in his black suit and thin gray tie. However, the pint of Jim Beam Holbert brought from under the left pocket of his suit jacket helped put them both at ease. It was then that Ron also realized his right arm was in a cast. The morphine had slowed him to this fact until the bourbon showed in his line of sight.

Maybe this guy isn't that big of a dick, Ron thought. *At least he knows what to drink.*

Holbert was accommodating. The seemingly good FBI boss poured a good inch of Jim Beam into a Styrofoam coffee cup before pointing a straw to Ron's lips. He added his own dram to another cup. They toasted and took a few minutes to enjoy the bourbon before getting to business.

"I need to get your take on a few matters," Holbert said. "Gino Drucci survived the improvised sting on his Lisle hideout, but we aren't getting any useful information that can be used against him in our federal investigation. The FBI appreciates any help you can give."

Much like their first meeting, Ron sensed something off about Holbert. He wondered why the man wasn't better at sweating out criminals who clearly deserved solitary confinement. He had to push back a little. Ron was bored, and pressing someone's buttons while drinking was a favorite way to amuse himself.

"How's Agent Russo doing?" Ron asked. "He seemed a solid character, and I haven't heard from him since the night we were working together to help out this so-called investigation. I assume that you've found him. Also, may I inquire where you were when the shit hit the fan at the hideout that you said was in Lisle? I was drugged and beat up soon after you and I last had the chance to talk."

"Mr. McCallister, I know that Agent Russo has vouched for your innocence in this case. He's also told us that your cooperation was fundamentally helpful. Was Russo wrong about your willingness to assist?"

"I'd like a lawyer present. I don't know any good ones off the top of my head, but I'm sure you might know quite a few."

"Ron, you're not under arrest. I am only asking for your assistance as a witness. That's the least you can do. Or am I wrong?"

Ron took a sip of his bourbon before answering. He didn't like the tone in the room but felt he didn't have much choice if he complained. The pager for the nurse was put out of reach sometime after Holbert had entered the room. He again hoped that the truth would be his best option.

He explained that Mike Simmons joined him and Carey Sullivan in suspecting that cocaine dealing and mob business were being protected by those associated with policing and governing Woolrich. Mayor Peck was probably doing business with Nicky Ferranti and others in the mob after the death of the previous mayor.

This made sense to Ron. Research at the public library and observations in the past few weeks validated his suspicions.

Ron suspected that the late Ferranti was behind the explosion at the Simmons household and Mike's death. The blast took care of the Mayor's troublesome insider. He was happy that Mike had sent his son, Brian, to stay with relatives. The mob would've considered Brian collateral damage, which only fortified Ron's desire to help Agent Russo take them down after they got in contact.

Ron hadn't expected Ferranti's assassination, but he suspected the mob was the main guilty party of that too. He didn't recognize the name Gino Drucci, but figured that he was a person of interest who had mob ties. He told as much to Holbert before he was faced with something else unexpected from his increasingly unwelcome company.

"I think you put too much faith in the mob," Holbert said. "The western suburbs' presumptive mob leader, Gino Drucci asked me and friendly stooges in the FBI to arrange the hit on Ferranti. Mayor Peck was on board as well, but Drucci will take the fall before the next wop interested in Woolrich arrives. Just as well, I'd like you to forget all this and make peace with whichever God you worship before becoming silent forever."

Ron saw the pillow going over his face before the world went black for the second time within within a week.

I'm really getting sick of this bullshit, he thought.

He fought against Holbert for breath. In his weakened state, Ron wasn't able to stave off the approach of impending death. He hoped for some help.

Hair of the Dog

Ron was more than a bit surprised when his eyes opened a few days later to the sight of Agent Matt Russo next to him in a pressed, black suit. From a marked calendar on the beige wall, it was the Tuesday after Sister Maria had visited him and the head of Chicago FBI had tried to asphyxiate him. Russo wasn't as pleasant a sight as Carey Sullivan or Sister Maria would have been. But Ron figured that at least he wasn't going to be choked or kidnapped. They had first met in the women's department of the Woolrich Walmart, but Ron grew to admire Russo as a tough and reliable guy.

"What the hell happened?" Ron asked him with lumbering breaths. "Why am I not dead? Last I remember, your boss put a pillow over my face after I filled him in on my take on the local mob scene."

"It turns out that my former boss, like your own, was a mob sell-out," Russo said. "Fortunately for you, Sister Maria wanted to keep an eye on you two after she noticed Holbert speaking Italian with some guy in the hallway. From the Latin she'd learned in the convent, she thought she heard something about 'killing the truth.' She was the one who kept you breathing after she pushed Holbert to the floor and yelled for the police."

Russo stopped when he saw a stone face of concern come over Ron.

"Fortunately, some legit local cops responded and arrested Holbert before any harm could come to Sister Maria."

"That's a relief," Ron said. "I suppose Woolrich's finest can handle a criminal. It just takes a nun to get the jump on him first. I knew I liked that lady for more than her kindness. She's smarter than any cop I've come across."

Russo gave a smile and chuckled, shaking his head before getting back to business.

"Later, I'll send in an FBI agent whom I've vetted to retake the statement that Holbert tried to suppress," he said. "In the meantime, the doctor told me to let you rest."

"You got any other good news for me?" Ron said. "Maybe a little whiskey for medicinal purposes? I just ask you don't try to kill me. I really wouldn't like that."

Russo motioned to a bored-looking police officer at the door. The blond crew cut on the round face nodded before the officer moved to vacate the doorway. A nurse pushed a wheelchair to transport Carey Sullivan next to Ron's bed. As soon as she could, she took Ron's hand and kissed it. She wiped some tears from her eyes as he took as deep a breath as he could and smiled from cheek to cheek.

"The vetted agent will take your statement after the doc gives us her permission," Russo said as he went toward the door. "She insists that she sign off before you can experience any more stress. I agree with her."

Ron gave a respectful nod to Russo as he left the room. Carey's son, John, soon joined the couple. All three hugged and Ron's face grew less taut and more colorful. He tussled John's hair with his left hand before the boy uttered a few words that made Carey and Ron smile.

"I like Ron," he said. "Mama and you keep safe."

Agent Russo kissed his wife, Clara, and daughter, Zoe, as he met them in the waiting room near the Woolrich Memorial ICU. That moment with his two ladies was the happiest he'd had in weeks. He needed a vacation, but the antiseptic ambiance around him reminded him of the work to be done.

In the previous week, he had issued arrests for Holbert's mob co-conspirators and watched his boss surrender to a federal holding facility. Rob Peck, Gino Drucci, and some mob underlings were well on their way to prison terms. He figured their convictions were just a matter of time with relevant surveillance, Mike's notes, and the testimonies from Ron, Carey, and Lizzy.

Agent Russo's immediate task was to attempt to interview a suspect who hadn't yet been jailed in Woolrich's latest controversy. Kendra De Silva was still being treated for drug withdrawal and a gunshot wound to her left leg. Sister Maria made it a personal mission to to help out the "lost child," but Russo had to start winding up his investigation with less regard to Kendra's long-term well-being.

He reluctantly excused himself from his family and went to Kendra's door.

"Ms. De Silva can see you now," said a nurse who stood outside.

He entered the room slowly. He wanted to make sure that Kendra had time to adjust. She was in a fragile state and he sensed she wouldn't react well to change or pressure. He was thankful to have some experience with forensic psychology.

"Hello, Ms. De Silva," Russo said. "I'm with the FBI. May I call you Kendra?"

"Mr. FBI," she replied, "you can call me whatever you want. What would you like me to call you?"

"You can call me Matt if you want to," he said. "May I ask you a few questions, Kendra?"

"What would you like to ask, Matthew?"

"I was wondering if you would talk about how things were going before you got to the hospital? Could you tell me more about what happened a week or so ago in Lisle?

Russo watched as her brow furrowed and she began to scratch quickly at scabs on her arms. He intervened by grabbing her hands with his. This sent a jolt of searing pain to his still-recovering right shoulder, which he suppressed through clenched teeth.

"Kendra, please... If you want to talk about something else, that's fine," he said after she had stopped struggling. "How are you sleeping?

"Matthew, come here and I'll tell you a secret."

Russo slowly drew near her side. He dodged when she ripped out an intravenous line from her arm and slashed toward him. He couldn't stop her before she took the needle and stuck it into her right carotid artery. He called for help as he put pressure on the wound. Hospital staff came quickly to stem the bleeding. Fortunately for Kendra, the suicide attempt happened very close to the emergency room. Staff quickly stopped the situation from escalating further.

Russo's face was pale as a nurse took him to a chair in a nearby room. His blood pressure and pulse were taken before he was given oxygen and checked for injuries. The nurse gave him a cold pack for his neck and a blanket to avoid shock.

Within an hour, Russo was cleared to change his shirt in the doctor's lounge. He took ten minutes to breath and stabilize himself enough to reunite with his family for the evening. He had to take Clara's shoulder to steady himself as they went to their black Ford Taurus.

I gotta get the hell away from the hospital, he thought. *Doctors, nurses, and psychotic witnesses are enough to make anyone claustrophobic*.

Clara drove him and Zoe to a Naperville Olive Garden so that they could try and relax over tortellini, decaf coffee, and endless cheap extras. Clara had a glass of Chianti. They didn't feel up to traveling to a decent Italian restaurant back in Chicago, and Zoe was happy to get all the cheap buttery bread sticks she could stand. After dinner, they found a room at a Comfort Suites before the Russo family could get a blissful, if short rest.

- - - - -

Agent Russo woke up before dawn the next morning and wandered into the parking lot of the motel. He joined a young woman who looked like a high school senior enjoying a cigarette. The gal released a cloud of smoke from her Parliament before introducing herself. The sun was starting to show itself in the eastern horizon.

"The name's Kate," she said with a bubbly voice. "I haven't been to the burbs since my folks took me out here for my tenth birthday. Seems kinda boring and a bit more clean than the city, but I'm still looking to show off my assets at a club in Woolrich. A girlfriend of mine says there's a lot of action there. You want a smoke, mister?"

He took the cigarette before giving her a

tight-lipped, stern-looking face he reserved for when Zoe was being stubborn.

"Are these guaranteed to kill me, Kate?" he asked. "If so, I could use one. I'm just leading an investigation into organized crime and drugs at a Woolrich strip club. If you're looking for a good way to shorten your own life, I'd take a Parliament over stripping and blow. But to each their own. Your parents know where you are?"

"For Christ's sake, you're a downer," Kate said. "Enjoy your damn cigarette. I'm going to go smoke by myself on the other end of the parking lot if you're going to be so depressing and boring."

Russo inhaled the dry carcinogens into his lungs as he stood alone. He held the smoke a few seconds before exhaling it into the atmosphere. His lungs burned, but the sensation was oddly pleasant. He closed his eyes and felt the orange rays of the emerging sun gradually warm the spring sky.

He enjoyed the complimentary breakfast with his wife and daughter a few hours after finishing his first cigarette in seven years, four months, and three days. The instant waffles and microwaved bacon were better than the smoke. He kissed his wife and daughter on their foreheads before they took their black Ford Taurus back to the city.

He dropped off his ladies at their home in the Logan Square neighborhood. He then had to check in at FBI Chicago headquarters due south in the Illinois Medical District. Duty called.

- - - - -

Agent Russo coordinated with the prosecution the Wednesday, Thursday and Friday before he took a week-long vacation. He worked three 16-

hour days before he left for the Bahamas. He was sure that a good friend of his, Federal Prosecutor Patrick Fitzgerald, would have a good start to putting the hammer down on Drucci, Peck, Holbert and any guilty subordinates.

It would be another career achievement for Patrick Fitzgerald. The prosecution of mobsters and their political cronies came nearly a year after his indictment of an adviser to Vice President Dick Cheney. After the long days, Russo mused to his friend that the criminality in politics organized crime was really only a difference of scale.

"Do you have enough to put these thugs away?" he asked Fitzgerald on a pay phone before he got on a flight with his family from gate B11 at O'Hare International Airport.

"Matt, these guys have more damning evidence than Scooter Libby, even though their mob connections don't reach to the White House," Fitzgerald said. "I think it's gonna be a slam dunk case unless someone with a billion dollars to their name comes to the rescue."

"You always got your fingers on the pulse of a case, Patrick," Russo said. "I'm sure my wife and I might be able to pick out something nice for you while we're out of the country."

"Why don't you pick out a few Cohibas for me?"

"I can probably do that and grab a few for myself as long as I don't get harassed by TSA or U.S. Customs hacks. You'll bail me out of jail, won't you Patrick?"

Russo's friend and colleague gave a chuckle that he read as jealous, yet jovial.

"Just don't mention my last name and we'll be fine. But on a more serious note, Matt, what kind of FBI agent doesn't know to properly smuggle contraband?"

28

A Fond Farewell

Ron, Carey, and her son, John, met with Aunt Peggy at Lavender Springs five days later in Naperville. They wanted to meet with her, and bring some Jameson to toast, before she took the opportunity to pass into infinity. Upon seeing her visitors, Aunt Peggy cried over the loss of her friend, Ervin, earlier in the week. After she cried for a while, Ron hugged her before she asked him to help her dry her eyes.

After he did, she looked at the couple and toddler attending to her with great interest.

"My dear nephew," she said. "You don't need my permission to be with this lass. I hope that you know that. I've always looked out for your best interests. My years of experience have given me the insight to see past all the politeness, pretension, and other hokum. You oughta stick with this gal."

Ron kissed his aunt on the cheek and hugged her. Her nearly translucent arms were unexpectedly strong. After a few minutes, he took Carey in his arms. He asked Carey to move in with him in Chicago while he worked things out with the FBI there. Aunt Peggy and John clapped as the two kissed and agreed. They'd have to see what their future held.

John sipped on a juice box while all the adults in the room toasted with two fingers of liquid gold. Aunt Peggy told more stories of growing up with Ron's mother in Cicero and said enough about raising Ron to make him blush. He responded with hearty chuckles, pouring both of them another dram.

"My work here is done for the lot of you," Aunt Peggy said before retiring. Carey and Ron hugged her before she went into a gentle slumber. A grin stretched from one of her cheeks to the other.

Later that evening, the Lavender Springs chaplain read Aunt Peggy her last rites and anointed her head before she passed away. Ron came to her side a short while before her death. He held onto her left hand with his right. He only released it when he needed to wipe away a few tears after she had gone.

Three days later, Ron, Carey, John, and several dozen people came out to pay respects for Aunt Peggy at a recently reopened St. John's Chapel. Some Lavender Springs staff and residents, distant family, and others she had helped during her meaningful life joined in a Catholic Mass that overflowed into Clarendon Hills Cemetery.

Everyone present joined in prayer or respectful silence to remember Aunt Peggy. It was the sendoff that she wanted.

After meeting those he recognized and others he should have gotten to know better, Ron broke down into tears after all the mourners left. John took his hand and helped him walk to Carey. They went to the Denny's where Delores worked. All three of them dined together as a nascent family. They left a generous tip.

29

Six Months Later

The Good Life

Ron McCallister kept up with Agent Matt Russo as they both aided prosecution of the Chicago mob's encroachment into the Western suburbs. Ron testified against the mob and politically-connected friends in Woolrich, happy to help justice clamp down on the dicks who tried to take down Carey, John, her friends, and him. His new FBI friend bought him at least two drinks at a bar of his choice after they spent days at Everett McKinley Dirksen United States Courthouse. It was a bonus he didn't take for granted.

After his last day of testimony, Ron made Russo pay for a cab to the California Clipper on California and Augusta in Chicago. They both enjoyed the old-fashioned, vinyl booths and the affable bartender, Kenny. The funky glow of neon red lights, the cheap drinks, and the fact that hipsters in nearby Wicker Park hadn't quite discovered it yet were also positive attributes. Bar-hoppers could always walk just over a mile northeast and pay twice as much on North and Damen.

"Jesus, it ain't even twilight yet and the two of you wanna get shit-faced," Kenny said between mixing a Rusty Nail and a Bloody Mary. "Ain't either of you got wives or lovers who smack you in your ugly mugs? By the way, you want the usual?"

The two nodded before Kenny's college-aged, half-Puerto Rican niece, Michela, brought Ron's

Sam Adams and Russo's Newcastle Brown. The left corner of her lips turned up in a grin before she winked at Ron and shook the curve of her behind. She had flirted with Ron before, but he had no intention of screwing up his life because a waitress liked to tease older men. Ron only tipped well and was courteous to Kenny's niece. It was the best way to conclude a productive number of weeks.

Ron and Russo both said Sláinte before draining their bottles by a fourth. Since the trial had begun, a number of mobsters and their collaborators were looking at prison. Gino Drucci and Dave Holbert were looking at possible life sentences. Rob Peck and several other thugs were looking at relatively lighter terms for crimes ranging from conspiracy to drug trafficking to accessory to murder. Kendra De Silva was able to serve as a witness after about two months of counseling. She was likely going to evade prison time because of her status as a minor during the crimes in question. Her cooperation with the prosecution and a good word from her social worker helped her situation.

"It's pretty amazing how the criminal justice system works when you are able to put some faith in it, Ron," Russo said. "By the way, if you need a job, I understand that the Bureau is looking for self-driven applicants with a college degree and a knack for investigation. You've done a hell of a job helping us in the burbs. Can you imagine getting paid to do such work?"

Ron finished his Sam Adams before answering.

"Matt, you've shown yourself to be an all-around nice fella," he said. "Don't risk our friendship and ask me to compromise my personal stance against authority. I would never join a bunch of assholes looking to make themselves look good on the taxpayers' dime. You and I are both veterans, so I'll cut you some slack."

Russo nearly spit out the rest of his beer before Ron told him to relax and flashed a shit-eating grin.

The FBI agent returned a tight-lipped, sardonic smile before speaking.

"It's a good day," he said after getting Michela's attention with the restrained manner of a high school science teacher wearing a freshly-starched plaid polo shirt. "Could you bring us over two Woodford Reserves, neat?"

She looked at him questioningly.

"That means no ice, hon," Ron said before he gave her polite grin. His company was about to protest when they were both served a five ounce glass full of the whiskey. Ron put a hand on his company's shoulder and smiled to Michela, asking for the check.

After the drink and some inebriated, friendly banter, Russo gave Michela a $15 tip before Ron paid the tab and led him toward the door of the California Clipper.

Ron called a cab from his Samsung flip phone. He gave the cab driver $20 and gave his FBI buddy's address. The money was worth more than twice the fare. Ron figured the hefty tip he gave the cab driver would guilt him into making sure his passenger got safely into the home he shared with his wife and daughter.

After drinking a glass of water back at the bar, Ron nodded to Kenny and walked nearly a mile north to the California Avenue station on the Chicago Transit Authority Blue Line El. From there, he spent just over $2 to ride toward O'Hare to get off at the Irving Park stop. The flat that he rented with Carey Sullivan was a three-block walk south.

The fifteen minute ride on the El helped further sober him before he made the short walk home. After checking on a sleeping John, he went to the next room, kicked off his shoes, and shrugged out of his khakis. He placed his white button-down on the floor before settling in next to Carey to get a pleasant rest.

- - - - -

Carey straddled Ron before dawn the next day. Her strong legs squeezed his ab muscles as he woke to the pleasant scene before him. The neckline of her robe allowed him to peek at her healthy cleavage as his hands reached for her upper thighs. He enjoyed her breasts and many other parts of her body before they were out of breath and the sun's rays started to illuminate their apartment.

"That beats the hell out of push-ups," Ron said as he lay next to her. She responded by wrapping her leg around his and stroking his chest. He kissed her neck and put a few loose strands of dark crimson hair behind her ear. Her soft breaths put him at rest.

After they lay nestled with her left arm draped over his chest for several hours, he unhurriedly got to his feet and donned shorts and a t-shirt before making them breakfast. He knew Carey needed to attend to John's needs in the nearby bedroom. He'd help out by making flapjacks and bacon before she brought in her boy. John came to the dining area dressed in Bob the Builder PJ's that "Uncle Matt" had bought for him.

Carey sat cross-legged in her robe at their makeshift dining table after starting coffee in their French press. John looked at comics in the *Sun-Times* as Ron dished up breakfast. It was a routine they enjoyed nearly every Saturday morning before Ron checked the classified ads for an honest job and looked after John as his mom worked.

Carey worked the night shift serving beer, wine, coffee, and cocktails at the Iguana Cafe off of Halsted and Grand. Delores hooked her up the job through a friend of a friend. It was a far classier joint than her stints at Woolrich establishments. Even though many of the clientele made less money than the average suburbanite, they tended to tip better. Also, the hours were better than a typical bar on weekdays.

"Carey, I've got something to ask you," Ron said as John took a bite of bacon and before she could get ready for work. "I know it's not going to be the easiest to answer and that your boy will always be the most important man in your life. He should be."

Carey kissed him on the cheek and told him to get on with his questions after she waved a tendril from her blushing cheek.

"I've been told I'm a good investigator, and I'm thinking I could go private. Some of Matt's friends, who've retired from the FBI, might be able to help me find inroads. Someone will have to look after John while both of us are busy with work. What do you think of hiring a babysitter to help out before John can attend preschool?"

"Well, I hoped you'd one day get off your ass and get a job," Carey replied. "We'll be able to find a caretaker for John, especially if you'll help pay. I was wondering if you had another question about our future."

"What did you have in mind?" Ron asked her with false sincerity.

"Oh, will you piss off if you don't know the question you should ask me?"

"Well, I wanted to ask you and John if it would be okay if we got married. Is that what you had in mind? Granted, you'll be family and I know that's a hard gig. Aunt Peggy'd been my only family until I found you two. I know it's not easy for a former stripper and a former bouncer to be good friends, let alone become family. Also, if you want me to look into a babysitter, I've got a friend in the FBI who can run really good background checks."

Carey gave him a jab to the gut before she kissed John and then him. Her lips lingered on Ron's before she whispered a yes. She then had to hurry to get ready. After fifteen minutes in the bathroom, she was washed, made-up, clothed in a black skirt and light blue button-down, and had her hair in a business-like clip. Ron smiled at her as she blew a kiss to her boys and whisked out the door with her purse and jacket.

Ron washed the dishes and cleaned pans before he got John and himself dressed and respectable-looking. Then they both took the El to the Chicago Cultural Center in the Loop. It felt somewhat odd for Ron to be holding a little hand and leading the son of his new fiancée, but he realized he was also comfortable. He never thought he'd be a father figure.

"You know you and I are family now, don't you?" he asked John as they rode the elevator to the top floor the Cultural Center. "If we want to overrule your mom, you're gonna have to work with me."

John only returned a grin and held his arms above his shoulders before Ron took hold of him and put his soon-to-be stepson on his shoulders.

They looked out at the high-rise buildings along Randolph paying homage to the market despite the faltering economy. The country had just elected its first black president. Despite any misgivings Ron held about politics, he couldn't help but be optimistic about the future.

Ron figured he would only be able to rely on the two remaining members of his family and one friend in the FBI to maintain the tenuous new balance in his life. The thought helped him feel content.

30

Loose Ends

After getting off work at two o'clock Sunday morning, Carey Sullivan got on the El at the Grand Blue Line stop and rode a nearly empty train to Irving Park. She felt okay about walking to the apartment she shared with Ron and her son thanks to the Beretta .22 compact handgun tucked in her purse. She yawned sleepily as she got to their front door. Ron greeted her at quarter to three and shushed her before leading them both into John's bedroom. She kissed her son on the forehead with a softness that didn't wake him. Ron led her into their bedroom, where he helped her remove her skirt, her blouse, and her bra before they held each other under the covers and let sleep overtake them both.

Carey woke about six hours later. She stealthily showered, put her red locks into a pony tail, and slipped into a gray pencil skirt and white blouse. Before she was able to sneak out the door, Ron drifted into their kitchen. He handed her a granola bar before she blew him a kiss.

She took the 53 bus south to the Pulaski Green Line stop. After transferring there, she took the El westward to the Oak Park stop and walked to St. Edmund's Parish. Although Carey hadn't been to a church since middle school, she promised to not be late for friends. She arrived just ten minutes before meeting Lizzy and her son, Brian, for Catholic Mass at at eleven thirty a.m.

Since Lizzy's stay at Woolrich Memorial Hospital, she had received much counsel from Sister Maria, who had been checking in with Ron,

Carey, and her. The empathetic, kind nun directed her eastward for work at Catholic Charities in Cicero, where she found administrative work. Two months after she had recovered in the hospital, she began renting an apartment in Chicago's western Forest Park suburb. She attended Mass with Brian weekly.

"Thank you for coming to join me," Lizzy said after the service was over. "I know it's your only guaranteed day off during the week. Let me treat you to coffee and a sandwich before you head home."

"It's my pleasure, Lizzy," Carey said. "I'm happy to see that you and Brian seem to have found a sense of peace. It looks like you like it here. Tell me, how is the job going?"

The three chatted and walked for several blocks before they found a Bruegger's Bagels. Brian asked to go in, telling Carey how much he loves the hot chocolate. Inside the franchise, they caught up over a simple but tasty lunch as Brian colored on scratch paper he got from a friendly barista. After an hour or so together, they hugged, smiled, and went their separate ways for the day.

- - - - -

Carey read the book, Elegance of the Hedgehog on the Green Line train toward downtown Chicago. She reflected on some similarities between the intelligent yet damaged heroines in the book and the women in her life. One of Carey's fellow waitresses at Iguana Cafe, who was Delores' friend of a friend, had lent it to her.

"It's sort of dry and a bit sad," the co-worker said, "but the message I took from it is that folks in the background are smarter than they let on.

Plus, there's some funny bits and a mysterious, handsome Japanese man."

Carey was indeed enjoying it. She was so wrapped up in the story that she almost missed her connection to the Blue Line subway at Clark and Lake in the Chicago Loop. After taking the escalators and descending the stairs, she was happy when the train came back above ground past Division Street. It was her favorite part of the trip to see the rooftops of three and four-flat buildings that had been transformed from residences to small businesses and local franchises in their hundred plus years of existence.

She turned back to her book as the train reverted to a subway near Logan Square before coming up for air near her apartment. The surroundings weren't as glamorous as downtown and other stops on the El, but it felt more like home. She was at ease walking the three blocks south with the sunshine of the late afternoon.

Ron and John met her at the door of their apartment as the inviting scents of Guinness, slow-cooked beef and rosemary floated to her button nose.

"John was preoccupied with his alphabet charts, so I decided to make Irish stew," Ron said. "I remembered that Aunt Peggy used to make it when the months started getting colder. Also, I found a recipe online using our neighbor's WiFi. It'll be ready in another hour or so."

Carey sat on the couch that came with their apartment and played alphabet games with John. Ron gave her a glass of red zinfandel as he checked on the meal. It gave off savory smells that peppered the air. As the hour hand on the living room clock hit six, he beckoned them to sit at the table.

Carey set out plates and silverware on their table, and they sat around and carried on like any other Midwestern couple who six months ago hadn't been in gunfights with the Chicago mob. After Ron filled her in on his and her son's adventures at the Cultural Center, she talked about her visit with Lizzy and Brian. She grew a little quieter when she thought about Lizzy adapting to the loss of her husband.

"You know that I'm still worried about the safety of my family," she said after sipping her wine. "If anything about our personal life leaks out from the press, gangsters will hear about it. You may have connections with the FBI, but I'm still worried about those mob thugs and their political pals."

"As long as there's a breath in my body, you two won't have to worry," he said. "You and I are both good shots. If we've learned anything from this past year, it's that we can survive. Also, I'm a hell of a cook."

They returned to their meal after he raised his wine and she returned a smile and a cheers. The lingering quiet between them was more from relaxation than worry.

After dinner, Ron taught John folk songs before his fiancée and her son got ready for bed. He tucked both of them in before kissing them on their foreheads. He cleared the kitchen, cleaned dishes and packed leftovers in Tupperware before pouring himself a finger of George Dickel No. 12 whisky.

Ron then alternated between worrying about his new family and reading portrayals about the darker side of humanity through a Mickey Spillane book. A second finger of Dickel calmed his nerves before he was harshly interrupted.

A call from a Russo's cell phone at quarter to eleven changed his immediate and future plans. He gulped down the rest of the whisky before he could spill it. He grabbed his Glock 9 mm and ran out the door to find a waiting cab on Irving Park.

- - - - -

The staccato blasts of gunfire weren't unusual from Agent Matt Russo's perspective. The first time he'd heard similar fire was when he shot targets at his uncle's hunting lodge in upstate New York. It was also a reminder of his days in Army boot camp and his subsequent first pump to Baghdad.

The first person he thought to call was Ron McCallister, who, despite hopping a cab and coming from over four miles northwest, was still faster than any policemen who could legally help him. The immediate problem for Russo was that he only carried his standard-issue Glock side-arm.

He immediately shot one of the men who happened to step out into the streetlight with a gun pointed at his home. He was pleased that he'd only incapacitated the goon, as intended. He didn't worry so much about where his shots landed when shooting at an attacker with an AR-15, whose blasts put holes in his wall. Russo aimed at the chest of the attacker with the semiautomatic assault rifle, stopping the stream of shots with two of his own.

Russo told his wife to take their daughter into the bathroom in the interior of their home, where no windows were open to outside gunfire. He hoped that she had taken his direction as a stray bullet from outside semiautomatic weapons fire lodged itself near his neck. It apparently hadn't hit his carotid artery because he could still shoot at the three assholes running across his lawn. He wasn't able to see Ron's cab before he lost consciousness.

The cab driver stopped a block from where gunfire was taking place on Logan Boulevard. He told Ron to get out, not bothering to collect his fare before frantically driving away.

Ron ran down the block with stealth and shot one of the three remaining attackers in the buttocks with his Glock before he took return fire. He ducked behind the back passenger's side of a new Volkswagen Beetle. The tiny car was obliterated in seconds with the staccato blasts of semiautomatics.

Two police cruisers arrived while Ron sprinted for cover and exchanged fire with two of the attackers. One of the thugs advanced toward the house and was soon shot in the lower back by a police officer. Ron dropped the other assailant with shots from his Glock before surrendering the handgun and his immediate freedom to police.

Another police officer went to check on Agent Russo's family as two EMT units arrived. One went into the Russo household while the other examined the gunmen who were incapacitated but not yet dead. Siren-sounding cars cleared the area before too many neighbors or press could ask questions.

The report from the press was that a gang shooting had left a local businessman and reputed mobster dead. A typical obituary followed in the *Tribune* and the *Sun-Times*. Few other questions were able to be asked. The Chicago Police Department, neighbors, the mob, and any family connected to the deceased were mum for the moment.

31

After the Chaos

Agent Matt Russo awoke in the intensive care unit of St. Mary Medical Center on Tuesday morning. The faces of his wife and daughter greeted him before an FBI agent and a U.S. Marshal identified themselves. Clara and Zoe kissed him on his stubbled cheeks before he put a few pointed questions to the FBI agent.

"Where's the asshole who shot me?" Russo asked. "Where is Ron McCallister? If you put him behind bars, you'll have more than hell to pay."

"Please remain calm, sir," the agent said. "You are all safe for now. After checking out Mr. McCallister's credentials, we saw the assistance he provided in prosecuting mob influence in Woolrich. We want to offer you both the chance to relocate and stay protected with your families in the Witness Protection Program."

Russo tried to get up, wanting to learn more about what was going on. His wife eased him back to a horizontal position before he could tear out any stitches. She gracefully ran her hands where his neck met his collar to remind him of his fragile condition. His fellow FBI agent continued.

"We've identified the attackers on your house as having connections to the Chicago mob. The man you shot while he was approaching your house was a longtime business associate of Gino Drucci and Joey Lombardo."

The agent explained that other thugs involved in Sunday evening's shooting had been suspected of laundering funds and other mob duties for the past decade. The agent also explained that these details wouldn't reach the press if Russo wanted witness protection.

"That everyday thugs are having to step up means that our boys in the Organized Crime Program are making mobsters feel desperate," the agent said. "Still, the fact that they attacked your home and Mr. McCallister's apartment shortly afterward makes the higher-ups want to put you in protection for the foreseeable future."

Russo blanched.

"For Heaven's sake, tell me that Carey and John Sullivan are okay," he said.

"Nothing's officially showed in the papers yet, sir," the agent said, "but Mr. McCallister explained to FBI Agents and Chicago Police that he woke up Ms. Sullivan with a cell phone call on the way to help you."

When police had finally arrived at Carey Sullivan's residence, the agent explained that they found that she had already shot and killed three intruders. Officers subdued another man who was later found to have connections with the thugs who shot up Russo's Logan Square home. The three deceased were found with their own handguns drawn, They received shots from a Beretta .22 compact that Sullivan later surrendered. They all died rather quickly from chest wounds.

Russo sdmirked at the news while Clara took his right hand and looked him in the eyes.

"That's all good news, I guess," he said, after nodding at his wife. "I don't really care what the higher-ups want, but I'll defer to my two ladies and hear what our pal in the U.S. Marshals Service has to say."

The fellow FBI agent stepped aside while the U.S. Marshal talked with him and his family about

WITSEC.

- - - - -

The following Sunday, Carey, John, and her fiancé, Ron rode the 53 bus south and the Green Line El west for eleven thirty a.m. Mass at St. Edmund's Parish. It was the last chance to see Lizzy and Brian Simmons before they left the area with help from the U.S. Marshals Service. Lizzy hugged them all before they sat down for Mass.

To Carey's content astonishment, Ron was able to explain much of the service to John when her son whispered questions. He whispered responses into her son's ear and whispered a few questions of his own. She was amazed at the level of engagement they held. She gave Ron a polite peck on the cheek during the sharing of peace.

He noticed her approving grin toward the end of Mass.

"Aunt Peggy tried to raise me right," Ron explained to her after the final song. "I hope I've done her proud by remembering something."

"I haven't a doubt," Carey said before taking his right hand with her left. John ran ahead with Brian under Carey and Lizzy's watchful gaze.

After shaking the priest's hand, the five went for coffee, hot chocolate, and sandwiches at Bruegger's Bagels. Carey wanted to deliver their news in a friendly place. She made sure that anything said would be discreet. The only other customers were out of earshot as she led them toward seats near the back exit.

"Lizzy, I have to tell you something, but it has to remain only with you until death," Carey said. "You're like a sister to me, so you're the only person with whom I share this in confidence. Can you understand?"

Lizzy sat up straight at their table and gave a solemn glance before swearing on her grave. She was about to make Brian take the same oath until Carey interrupted and took her hands. Brian ignored the seriousness and sipped his hot chocolate, making faces with John.

"My fiancé, my son, and I have to change our identities and leave town with WITSEC protection due to how much we know about Chicagoland crime. I won't tell you where we are going except that we won't be in the continental United States. I won't be able contact you for at least a few months. Officially, I am not able to talk to you again, but I was never one for following all the rules."

Lizzy nodded her head in understanding. She took looked into Carey's eyes to show she could be trusted. She gave the same look to Ron and flashed a smile at John.

"You must tear up and dispose of the note that I'm about to give you immediately after you've read it. It will be our Skype identification after we move," Carey whispered in her friend's ear. "You must understand that this otherwise unidentifiable name will be only known to you so that we can get in touch with you alone."

Lizzy nodded before taking the note, memorizing the name, and tearing the note into a number of pieces before putting the pieces in Ron's coffee. She gave him a sardonic grin.

Ron gamely smiled before took a big swig of the coffee, careful not to swallow pieces of the torn note. Carey, John, and he left in silence after a half hour of lighter talk. Carey nudged her friend's shoulder and tousled Brian's hair before they left. Ron got rid of the remnants of the note in a public waste basket on the way to the Green Line El.

Lizzy and Brian stayed at the table to finish a crossword. They left Bruegger's an hour later. She smiled at the thought that her friend placed such faith in her. As she walked with her son to their decade-old Saturn SL2, she swore that she wouldn't betray that faith.

Epilogue

Four Months Later

La Buena Vista

The golden hues of the sun lit Ron's shaven face as he looked out at the Caribbean. He sipped the mixture of rum, mint, and lime as he finished barbecuing ribs and plantains for dinner. His wife, Carey, joined him after she had mixed another round of mojitos for the two of them. She gave orange juice with a bit of mint to their son.

It was the Sunday before St. Patrick's Day, and he and Carey were enjoying the climate despite the lack of Guinness or whiskey. Fajardo, Puerto Rico gave them all a welcome change from the freezing temperatures in Chicago. Leaving home in the middle of January had been good timing.

The 80 degree weather allowed Carey to set their table outside. Also to Ron's enjoyment, the warmth of the early evening allowed his wife to tie only a lime green tie-dye sarong over her black one-piece swimsuit and call herself dressed. He smiled as he noticed her muscular right thigh peak out a casual slit. He had to clear his mind of some distracting thoughts before leading John toward a water fountain to wash for dinner. The boys both donned matching white *guayaberas* over their pale blue board shorts to appear somewhat respectable.

The day off allowed a brief respite for the Rileys, which was Ron, Carey, and John's new last name after their marriage and entry into WITSEC at the beginning of 2009. Over the last months, they were becoming acquainted to their new identities, professions, and environment. Ron and Carey had both found new lines of work and could occasionally drive to check in to the FBI office just over an hour west in San Juan.

Carey worked at a local firing range for police and gun clubs. The director of the range was impressed with her marksmanship and gave her a job despite her being a *mujercita*, a little woman. Ron tended bar at a watering hole in Luquillo to the West and regularly kept up with information on drugs and local organized crime. Every once in a while he passed on a little to a *policía* he had befriended if he felt it would spare innocent lives. Ron and Carey both worked in more satisfying jobs, and the tropical climes and beach house only made them more content.

John was having a bit of trouble with authority at preschool, but he didn't seem worried about that as he ate up the bits of rib that Ron had cut for him. Ron had no problems with his step-son's rebelliousness, either. But Carey's resistance made them both try to fit in more.

They were all picking up Spanish splendidly. Ron had already learned some Spanish from fellow soldiers in the Army. Both him and Carey heard a variety of of curse words and basic greetings when they worked at Starlet's Alley.

Carey thought about her friends, Lizzy and Brian often. She hoped to be able to connect with them at some point. She figured that her friend was reliable and would make contact in due time. She wouldn't let worry interrupt the present with her two boys.

When they finished the dinner of sweet plantains and barbecue, their part of the world rotated out of view of the sun. Carey and Ron cleaned the table and tucked John into bed before they sat in front of their home and gazed at the almost full moon.

Ron sipped Jim Beam on a few ice cubes and put an arm around his wife's shoulders. Carey rested her Bacardi on the rocks on her lap and tickled his left calf muscle with her right foot. He tickled her below her ribs until her healthy bosom bounced with laughter. When she regained her breath, she leaned back and spoke.

"I'm glad we can still have fun after all the drama we've dealt with."

"Well, I'm more a doer and a fixer than a poet," he said. "But Victor Hugo, who is much better with words, said 'laughter is the sun that drives winter from the human face.'"

Carey was silent as Ron's face remained taut as if he were trying to suppress a grin. She caressed the nape of his neck and he noticed her crossing her legs.

"Where did that come from, dork?" she asked.

"An English teacher gave me the quote my first year of college. I'd tell you it came from a fortune cookie at a Chinese chop suey restaurant, which would be funnier if it was true. But for now, I'll just say it's a good piece of advice."

"Ron, you worry about tarnishing your tough guy image, but I know that you are actually emotionally fuzzier than a rainbow-colored panda who is looking to mate and start a family."

He smiled and kissed her on the lips before she continued.

"I mean, you have the most wonderful thing a former bouncer could say to a former stripper. You're more marshmallow than Norman Mailer, but you're still a hard nut to crack. Chicks dig that.”

He groaned in amusement and passion before he tickled her belly and kissed her on the forehead. She gave him a sharp, but playful punch to his firm gut.

“I'm more solid that I've been in a long time,” he said. “That doesn't mean I can't get emotional from time to time. You of all people should know that.”

Carey kissed him on the lips and they returned to sipping spirits and letting their senses take in the light of the moon, framed by various shades of blue.

After about an hour of watching the sky and listening to the ocean gently lap the shore, they took each others' hands and tucked in for a good rest. Carey wrapped her leg around Ron before their eyes closed. He realized he'd found home in spite of himself.

- - - - -

Two men were watching Ron and Carey later that Monday morning. Neither made a sound as Carey headed to her job and they followed Ron as he chaperoned John's walk to school. After Ron left John at the school and before he'd head to his job in Luquillo, they'd deliberately make their move.

Acknowledgments

A Racket in the Burbs wouldn't have been possible without the help of family and good friends. First and foremost, I thank my wife, Caroline, for her patience, support, and assistance editing and brainstorming. She is a constructive critic, a competitive cribbage opponent, and a great partner.

My good friend, Mark Marohl, was the first person other than myself, who read an extremely rough draft of this story. I thank him for his encouragement and comments on many of my writing projects.

Two of my cousins were particularly helpful with language and adding authenticity to this story. Cody Broeren, a veteran of the U.S. Marine Corps, helped with military jargon and input on various action sequences. José Roberto Sánchez gamely answered questions regarding Spanish translation and Puerto Rican culture. Thank you both. I take responsibility for any potential errors.

I want to extend my appreciation to workers of the Chicago Public Library for a number of online and other resources. Libraries in general are a wonderful resource for communities to invest in knowledge and understanding, the local economy, entertainment, and other social goods.

Thank you also to booksellers everywhere, whether at local independents, national chains, or local franchises. You help spread the joy of reading and storytelling even when your days are the most frustrating.

Lastly, many thanks for the encouragement of my folks, Marcia and Dale, and my large extended family.

About the Author

Ben Broeren is a native of Wisconsin and has a BA in Sociology and an MA in Journalism from the University of Wisconsin-Madison. He has worked many jobs, including washing dishes and cooking at a Japanese Restaurant, advocating and working with disabled adults, office temping, selling stories at a bookstore, and volunteering in various political and social causes. He gained invaluable writing advice as a freelance reporter for newspapers and alternative weeklies in Chicago and Madison, Wisconsin.

He currently lives with his wife, his son, and his dog in the Bridgeport neighborhood of Chicago. When not writing and editing, he likes to cook various types of cuisine, read, teach young writers, ride his recumbent trike, and keep up with what's going on in the world through the news and conversing with neighbors.